A Wedding in New York

You are cordially invited to the wedding of the century...

Heiress Ivy Jenkins and CEO Sebastian Davis—Manhattan's It Couple!—are set to tie the knot at New York's *ultimate* wedding venue: Parker & Parker.

With their guest list a who's who of the city's A-Listers, Ivy and Sebastian want a wedding to remember! So they need the best in the business to help plan their perfect day... Cue Alexandra Harris, Hailey Thomas and Autumn Jones! The wedding planner, florist and maid of honor may be there to make Ivy and Sebastian's day magical... but what if their love lives receive a sprinkle of Christmas magic, too?

Discover Alexandra and Drew's story in

The Wedding Planner's Christmas Wish
by Cara Colter

Hailey and Giovanni's story in

Prince's Christmas Baby Surprise by Ellie Darkins

and

Autumn and Jack's story in

Reunited Under the Mistletoe by Susan Meier

Available now!

Dear Reader,

I love writing Christmas stories. Toss in Manhattan and a wedding and there's even more fun.

Ivy and Sebastian are society darlings. The venue for the wedding is to die for. With millions of dollars at my imagination's disposal, I could have just about anything I wanted for that wedding. Fancy food. Eye-popping decorations. Limos. Tuxes. Gowns. I had it all to play with.

But in the background hums another story. Jack Adams also has it all. But he's alone. Bridesmaid Autumn Jones and her family tempt him to want something more.

The clock is ticking. Jack and Autumn have one month of wedding planning and working together on Autumn's interview skills before they'll go their separate ways.

Can she convince him his life is in the future, not the past?

Susan Meier

Reunited Under the Mistletoe

Susan Meier

Special thanks and acknowledgment are given to
Susan Meier for her contribution to the
A Wedding in New York miniseries.

H HARLEQUIN®

Romance™

Recycling programs
for this product may
not exist in your area.

I3DN 13: 978-1-335-40688-0

Reunited Under the Mistletoe

Printed in U.S.A.

Susan Meier is the author of over fifty books for Harlequin. *The Tycoon's Secret Daughter* was a Romance Writers of America RITA® Award finalist, and *Nanny for the Millionaire's Twins* won the Book Buyers Best Award and was a finalist in the National Readers' Choice Awards. Susan is married and has three children. One of eleven children herself, she loves to write about the complexity of families and totally believes in the power of love.

Books by Susan Meier

Harlequin Romance

A Billion-Dollar Family

Tuscan Summer with the Billionaire
The Billionaire's Island Reunion

Christmas at the Harrington Park Hotel

Stolen Kiss with Her Billionaire Boss

The Missing Manhattan Heirs

Cinderella's Billion-Dollar Christmas
The Bodyguard and the Heiress
Hired by the Unexpected Billionaire

Visit the Author Profile page
at Harlequin.com for more titles.

CHAPTER ONE

"THE QUEEN SENDS her regrets."

The Queen?

Autumn Jones stifled a laugh. She knew Ivy Jenkins's society wedding would be packed with a who's who of guests...but the Queen?

She glanced around the office of Ivy's Park Avenue townhouse. Decorated for Christmas, the whole place could have been taken from the pages of a high-end style magazine because Ivy was Manhattan royalty. Autumn, the most average woman on the face of the earth with her mid-length auburn hair and hazel eyes, should have felt out of place, but because of Raise Your Voice, the charity where Ivy volunteered and Autumn worked, she and Ivy had become close. Not just friends. More like sisters.

As Ivy's assistant handed a Tiffany's box to her, a gift in lieu of the Queen's appearance, dark-haired, green-eyed Ivy arched one perfectly shaped eyebrow. "She's seriously not coming? Are you kidding me?"

This time Autumn couldn't hold back the laugh. Sometimes Ivy's life amazed her. "You weren't actually expecting *the* Queen to come to your wedding?"

"No. I just thought she'd RSVP by the November twenty-eighth deadline. Not two days after. For Pete's sake, where is her staff?" She pointed at the seating chart she and Autumn had been reviewing in front of a marble fireplace rimmed with evergreen branches and bright red ornaments. "Look, she has a seat...two. One for her. One for her guest. Because Alexandra, the wedding planner, made this chart based on RSVPs."

Autumn shook her head. It was exactly two weeks until the wedding and though Ivy was as polished as ever, her nerves were beginning to fray. Not a lot. She'd been one of Manhattan's elite her entire life. She knew how to be a lady, and she liked to throw a party—two reasons why Autumn and Ivy had bonded at Raise Your Voice, a charity created to assist underprivileged women who needed help climbing the ranks of corporate America. Ivy had the connections and Autumn had the skills to host events that raised millions.

As Ivy handed the Tiffany's box back to her assistant who walked it to the table with the other wedding gifts, the office door opened again. Sebastian Davis, CEO of one of New York's most exciting tech startups and Ivy's fiancé, entered.

Wearing a dark suit and white shirt with a thin gray tie, he looked ready for the board meeting Autumn knew he had that crisp Saturday.

"Good morning, everybody."

Ivy and Autumn said, "Good morning."

He bent down and bussed a quick kiss across Ivy's cheek. "More gifts?"

Ivy rolled her eyes. "And late RSVPs. We're looking at the seating chart before I approve it for Alexandra." She took a quick breath. "Did you know the Queen wasn't coming?"

He winced. "No. But it takes a lot to get her to travel to America these days. Besides, the royals from Adria are coming. That's enough royalty for anybody's wedding." He headed for the door again. "I'll see you at dinner." But he stopped suddenly and pivoted to face them. "By the way, Autumn, your partner for the wedding is having dinner with us tonight and I was hoping you would join us."

Ivy clapped. "Oh, great idea!" She turned to Autumn. "I cannot wait for you to meet Jack."

Autumn happily said, "Okay. I don't think I have plans on my calendar for tonight, but even if I do, I'm sure I can reschedule. Anything you need in the next two weeks, I'm your girl."

"Good," Sebastian said.

Ivy smiled.

She rose from her chair, grabbing her purse

and briefcase from the floor beside it. "I should get to work, too."

Sebastian waited for her at the office door. "You're going into your office on a Saturday?"

"Most of our clients have Monday through Friday jobs. Saturdays are when they have time for appointments with our mentors."

Sebastian smiled. "Makes sense. Can I give you a lift?"

"No. I'm fine."

They walked into the main foyer, a space so elegant it could have been in a museum. The sound of their heels clicking on the marble floor echoed around them.

Sebastian opened the black and etched glass front door for her. She stepped out with a murmured, "Thanks," for Sebastian, but when she looked toward the street, she blinked and did a double take.

Leaning against Sebastian's black limo was a big, fat unresolved piece of Autumn's past—

Jack Adams.

Tall and thin and wearing a dark suit and black overcoat in the cold last-day-of-November air, he looked every inch a mogul like Sebastian.

His blue eyes met hers across the sidewalk. He pushed off the fender of the limo.

Sebastian said, "Hey! You're here!"

"I wanted to catch a ride to the board meeting.

Thought I could run my new management system by you while we drove."

Sebastian motioned to the car. "Great. Get in." Then he faced Autumn. "Autumn, this is Jack Adams, your partner for the wedding."

Jack held her gaze. He didn't make a move to tell his friend Sebastian they already knew each other. In fact, he extended his hand to shake hers, like they were strangers meeting for the first time.

Oh, dear God! Maybe he didn't remember her!

"Jack, this is Autumn Jones."

Their hands met, wrapped around each other and bobbed up and down once. Feeling like a deer in the headlights, Autumn could only stare at him. She'd think she had the wrong guy—Jack Adams was a common name—but she'd remember those blue eyes anywhere. Five years had been very kind to him. Not only did he appear smooth and polished, but also he was just plain gorgeous.

In that second, she could forgive herself for their one-night stand. Because had it been up to her, it would have been more than a one-night stand. But looking at him now, she could see why he hadn't thought of her as anything other than a passing fancy.

He was well dressed, sophisticated, obviously rich.

And she was still Autumn Jones, outreach officer for Raise Your Voice. She had the same car, same apartment, same job… Good God. It was like she was stuck in a time warp.

"It's nice to meet you Mr. Adams…"

He almost smiled. "Jack."

Or maybe he did remember her?

Her heart thrummed as she recalled some particularly *interesting* parts of their encounter.

A blush crept up her cheeks. "Sure. Sure. Jack."

Sebastian said, "Sorry, Autumn. Don't mean to rush off but we've got to get going."

"Me too." She pointed to the right. "I'm picking up a birthday cake at the bakery—"

Her voice trailed off and she fought to keep her eyes from squeezing shut in misery. Her biggest claim to fame was that she was the office birthday girl. She remembered the date, bought the cake, got the card signed.

No fancy job. Not married. Not dating. Still ten pounds overweight.

Yeah, Fate. She got it. No sense in rubbing salt into the wound.

She pivoted to head to the bakery.

"Nice to meet you, too, Autumn."

Jack's smooth voice stopped her dead in her tracks as it washed over her like good whiskey. Which, if she remembered correctly, had been his drink of choice.

Refusing to think about that night, that wonderful night that could have stayed in her memory like the plot of a favorite movie if he hadn't unceremoniously disappeared from her bed, she faced him again.

She said, "Thanks," then quickly turned to go.

Before she got two steps down the block, Sebastian called, "Don't forget dinner tonight!"

This time she did squeeze her eyes shut. Seriously? She had to endure dinner with him? She groaned. And the *entire* day of the wedding?

She straightened her shoulders. Damned if she'd let that hurt or upset her. She might be stuck in the past, but she was a mature adult. And no matter how successful he was, he was an oaf. He'd swept her off her feet then sneaked out in the middle of the night. No goodbye. No call the next day. Or the next week. Or the next month.

Yeah. She was over him.

She popped her eyes open then faced Sebastian and Jack again with a smile. "I won't forget!" she said with a wave, hoping to speedily spin around and get out of there—

But her eyes met Jack's and she suddenly felt tall and why-hadn't-she-ever-buckled-down-and-lost-those-ten-pounds? clumsy.

Damn it! What the hell was it about this guy that she couldn't step out of idiot mode?

Waking up in her empty bed the day after the most romantic night of her life had been embarrassing and soul crushing, but she'd moved on.

Really.

Seeing him shouldn't even be a blip on her radar screen!

But if the tightening of her chest was anything to go by, it hadn't quite been the nonevent she'd convinced herself it was.

She said, "Goodbye," pivoted and raced away, her heart heavy.

Yeah. It truly hadn't been the nonevent she'd convinced herself it was.

Jack Adams stared out the darkened window of Sebastian's limo.

Of all the people to be his partner for Sebastian and Ivy's wedding… Autumn Jones? The woman who reminded him of the worst day of his life?

"You wanted to talk about your new management system?"

"Not really the system itself," he said, glancing at Sebastian. "The provider. I've got it narrowed down to three. I wanted to see if you'd heard of any of them."

Sebastian chuckled. "You mean you wanted to see if I knew any dirt on any of them."

Jack snorted. "Yeah."

"Okay, who are you considering?"

Jack opened his briefcase and handed Sebastian his short list.

Sebastian scanned it. "Two are relatively new.

But this one," he said, pointing at a name on the list, "has been around forever. That's always a nudge in their favor…"

"That's the group we were thinking about working with." Jack put the list back in his briefcase.

"So, you're good?"

"Yeah, I'm good."

Sebastian eyeballed him. "You don't look good. You look like you swallowed a live fish."

Jack gaped at him. "A live fish?"

"Yeah. Something that didn't go down well."

This was why Sebastian was rolling in success. A genius with a keen business sense wasn't unheard of. A genius who could read people like short books? Not so easy to find.

"Maybe I'm just making too big of a deal about the management system. After all, there are prepackaged systems for restaurants…especially companies with multiple sites."

"Or maybe you're avoiding the subject."

Jack reached for a bottle of water from the small fridge beside the limo's minibar. There was no way he'd tell Sebastian about his night with Autumn. Partially because he didn't want to embarrass her. Partially because it had taken him years to erase that night from his brain. He didn't want to bring it up again.

"You know that anybody who runs a com-

pany is always thinking. Always preoccupied."
He opened the water and took a long drink.

"Yeah, I get it." Sebastian nudged Jack's bicep.
"But how about being present tonight. Who
knows? You might just hit it off with Autumn."

Jack swallowed so hard and so fast, he almost
choked. "She seems like a very nice woman but..."

Sebastian frowned at Jack. "But what? She's
not your type?"

"I don't have a type."

"Of course, you do. Cool brunettes who don't
ever really get to know you because they're shal-
low and you pretend to be somebody else. And at
least two of them were crazy."

"That's not true."

Sebastian only looked at him. "Not even the
one who stole from you? Or the one who burned
down your beach house?"

Jack grimaced. He had horrible luck choosing women. Everyone but Autumn because she'd
only been a one-night stand. She hadn't had time
enough to do something egregious like steal
from him, cheat on him or burn down his beach
house—

Which was why he now only had one-night
stands. He'd gotten engaged three times out of
a desperate need to feel connected, to feel normal, to have a normal life. He was over that now.
Some people simply were made to stand alone.

Be strong. Make their mark as a businessperson, not a family man.

"All right. It's a little true. But I finally figured out it's not a good idea for me to settle down. There are temptations in a billionaire's life." Like things to steal. "And I work hard." Leaving at least one fiancée so lonely, she'd cheated.

Sebastian snorted. "And fiancée number three had a temper."

He held back a groan. She sure had. A person had to be really angry to pour gasoline on someone's sofa, toss a match on it and walk away without a backward glance. "Yeah. She had a temper."

"But I do agree that you work hard. Maybe too hard."

"Probably." But he worked hard for his mom. For her vision. To see that vision realized. She'd come up to him the night of his first and only Raise Your Voice gala and told him she wasn't feeling well and would be taking the limo home. He thought of going with her, but he had already spotted Autumn across the room and felt like lightning had struck him. So, he'd kissed his mom's cheek and let her go.

Then he'd turned off his phone and eased through the groups gathered in the crowded ballroom to introduce himself.

While he and Autumn were laughing, dancing and eventually going back to her apartment, his mom had realized she was having a heart attack, called an ambulance, gotten herself to the hospital and ultimately died.

Seeing Autumn reminded him of his biggest failure, his greatest mistake. If getting engaged to a thief, a cheater and a woman who burned down his beach house had been bad, losing his mom because he's been bedazzled by a woman had been the worst.

He'd be a mature adult and do his part for Sebastian's wedding, but he'd limit the time he spent with Autumn. If only to keep her in the category of one-night stand and not give her the chance to prove yet again that he wasn't a good judge of women and shouldn't have relationships.

He also didn't need to be reminded that Autumn had started his run of bad luck with women.

CHAPTER TWO

AUTUMN PULLED FOUR DRESSES from her closet, looking for something to wear to dinner. She didn't want to dress up, but she also didn't want to look out of place. Normally with an impromptu invitation she'd go home with Ivy, borrow something to wear and dress at her house. Easy-peasy.

Angry, confused, and even a little confused about why she was so angry, she couldn't risk slipping something to Ivy about Jack—*the guy who'd pretended not to know her.* Her best friend was getting married. She didn't want to spoil anything about the next two weeks for Ivy. So, she couldn't tell her about Jack dumping her. She had to look normal. Happy.

On the other hand, she didn't want Jack Adams to think she'd dressed up for him. The scoundrel. Make love to her as if she was the woman of his dreams then never call? It would be a cold, frosty day in hell before she'd dress up for him. It would be difficult enough to speak civilly to the oaf.

In the end, she chose a simple black dress, high

heels and a sparkly clutch bag that she'd gotten at a secondhand store. She left her apartment, raced to the subway, and headed for the Upper East Side and Ivy's townhouse again.

Jack exited his limo and told the driver to return for him in two and a half hours. He was tired after the board meeting that had taken an entire day. But he also knew Sebastian and Ivy would be tired. Not only had Sebastian been with him at his board meeting, but he and Ivy were knee-deep in exhausting wedding preparations. He wouldn't overstay his welcome.

Climbing the steps to the townhouse, he also wouldn't let himself think about Autumn. Though he knew she was probably tired too if she'd spent the day at her office, he couldn't handle the feelings that rumbled through him just recalling her name. Anger with himself and grief had almost paralyzed him that day. He couldn't let seeing her bring all that up again.

He rang the bell and Ivy's longtime butler answered. "Good evening, sir."

"What's on the menu tonight, Frances?" Jack asked as he shrugged out of his overcoat and handed it to butler.

"Seared steak and polenta with *chimichurri*."

His mouth watered. "Ah. Is Chef Randolph tonight's chef?"

"Yes. It's Louis's night off. Randolph asked about you. Maybe you could stop by and say hello after dinner."

"I'll do that."

Frances took the overcoat. "Everyone's in the drawing room."

He smiled at Frances, straightened his jacket and tie and headed into the second room on the right. As soon as he stepped over the threshold, he saw her. Tall and shapely in her black dress with her shoulder-length reddish-brown hair curled in some kind of foo-foo hairdo, she looked amazing. Feminine, yet sophisticated.

Sebastian rose from the sofa. "There he is."

Jack glanced at his watch. "I'm not late, am I?"

"No. No!" Ivy reassured as she walked over to give him a hug. "We're just happy to see you."

He shook Sebastian's hand, then—obligated to do so by social convention—he turned to Autumn. "Good evening, Autumn."

She politely said, "Good evening," from her Queen Anne chair across from the sofa. The room had been decorated for the holiday with red and green ornaments nestled in evergreen branches. They sat on the mantel, looped over drapes in the big window and hugged the bases of lamps.

Sebastian walked to the bar. "What can I get you to drink?"

"Whiskey."

Autumn shot him a glance. She knew he drank whiskey. They'd had a night together. She *knew* things about him. Personal, intimate things. Like his ticklish spots. She'd laughed at them…then ran her tongue along them to make him crazy.

He took a cleansing breath. That morning, it had been easy to pretend he didn't know her. To-night, it sat like a four-ton elephant in the center of the room. Something he and Autumn would have to walk around. Something Sebastian and Ivy would trip over.

Of course, they wouldn't know it. They could say a million embarrassing things, but as long as he and Autumn ignored them, everything would be fine.

Ivy said, "I heard your board meeting went well today."

Jack snorted. "Depends on your perspective. I prefer two-hour board meetings to eight-hour board meetings."

Sebastian handed Jack his whiskey. "Then you shouldn't want to expand and need the advice of your board. A board you chose I might add."

Autumn gave him a sideways glance. "The board meeting this morning was for *your* company?"

Pain rippled through him. Any time anyone called Step Inside *his* company, it was like a knife in his chest. Step Inside had been his mother's dream. His mother's baby. Now he was running it, shaping it, enjoying the benefits of its success.

Still, he faced Autumn with a smile, not showing one iota of emotion. "Yes. We were working out details for expanding." Quickly, to prevent Sebastian from telling Autumn things Jack preferred to stay private, he added, "The original five-year plan finishes in six months, and today I was seeking approval and guidance for expansion in the next five years."

"Your plan is ambitious," Sebastian said. "But I've seen you in action. You can do just about anything you put your mind to."

"Interesting," Autumn said. "In other words, if he sets his mind on something, something he really wants...he goes after it?"

"Yes!" Sebastian wholeheartedly agreed.

Jack worked to stay tall in his chair and not slink down in embarrassment. She clearly assumed he hadn't been interested in her after their one-night stand and that was why he hadn't called her. Which was okay. He'd take the hit. From her vantage point, he had treated her terribly. But hearing her say it, backhandedly calling him out, he had to struggle not to wince.

He'd always believed Autumn had been the first in his string of bad choices about women... so why did he suddenly feel like the villain?

Autumn said, "That's wonderful."

Before she could ask him another question or toss a barb, he smiled and said, "What about you, Autumn? You work at Raise Your Voice, right?"

She cleared her throat. "Yes."

"That's an interesting charity."

She pulled in a long breath. Her expression became like a thundercloud, as if he'd somehow insulted her.

Ivy said, "She's the go-to girl for everything. She manages their PR and is the public face of the company. She organizes most events. She supervises staff *and* the mentors who have 'office' hours on Saturdays."

A bit surprised, he peeked over at Autumn. They'd spent most of their night together dancing and making love, but he did remember she had organized the gala where they'd met.

A blush crept up her cheeks. Was she embarrassed?

In the five years since they'd seen each other, he'd taken over a company and she was still in the job she'd said was a steppingstone to—

He'd forgotten what it was a steppingstone to, but as he looked into her pretty hazel eyes, more memories formed. He remembered her in bed, naked with a tousled mess of sheets covering bits and pieces of her legs and torso, her eyes shining as she talked about things she wanted out of life. Happiness first and foremost, but also the kind of position that would come with respect.

Since she was still in the same job, he supposed the *respect* aspect of her future might not have materialized.

But all those mundane recollections were edged out by the memory of how soft she was. How touching her had felt like coming home. How she kissed in a way that made him feel he was sinking into something important.

He shook his head to dislodge the images. Those were the things that he couldn't let himself think about. Not merely to prevent the next thoughts—the phone call that woke him, racing to the hospital and being told his mother had died—but also so he wouldn't wonder what might have been.

Like the Prince in *Cinderella*, he'd felt he'd found something special, maybe even the woman of his dreams, but he'd been the one to race away and go back to his real life. Not that it was drudgery—

Frances stepped into the wide doorway. "Dinner is served, ma'am."

Sebastian rose and took Ivy's hand to help her stand. "Thank you, Frances."

With a quick nod of acknowledgment, the butler left.

Sebastian motioned Autumn and Jack to the door. As the foursome walked down the hall to the elaborate dining room that had been decorated with tinsel, and shiny red ornaments, Jack wasn't sure what to do with his hands. Should he guide

Autumn to the dining room with a hand on the small of her back? Should he keep his distance?

In the sitting room, actually talking to Autumn, too many memories had assaulted him. Good and bad. Happy and devastating. It was no wonder he'd forgotten common courtesy.

Sebastian seated Ivy. Jack followed suit and seated Autumn, who cast him a confused look. He wanted to tell her he was simply following Sebastian's lead not getting familiar, but that would break their cover.

He took the chair beside Autumn, across from Ivy and Sebastian who had chosen the more intimate seating arrangement rather than sitting at the head and foot of the long table.

Ivy smiled. Looking elegant and sophisticated in her slim red dress and pixie haircut, she lit the room. "No more talk of business. No more talk of companies. We want you and Autumn to get to know each other."

He glanced at Autumn, who smiled at Ivy. "Oh, I think we know each other well enough to be partners in a wedding."

Jack fought back a wince.

"Let's talk about something more interesting than me and Mr. Adams."

The insult of her use of his formal name rumbled through him and he quietly said, "Jack. My name is Jack. Remember?"

She turned and smiled, but if the woman wanted to be on Broadway, she'd never make it. Her smile was so fake it was a wonder her face didn't crack.

"Of course, *Jack*."

Until that moment, he'd never looked at their one-night stand from her perspective. First, he'd been grieving his mom. Then he'd been busy. Then he'd had a string of terrible engagements that had rendered him totally incapable of having a relationship. But tonight, he suddenly realized he'd hurt her.

And why not? They had been like soul mates who'd found each other after a long separation. They'd instinctively known each other's whims and wishes—

Then he'd never called.

A thought hit him like a boulder falling on a road in the Rocky Mountains.

What if that night hadn't just been the worst night of his life?

What if his not calling had made it the worst night of hers?

What if she wasn't the first in his string of bad encounters with women but the last in his string of good encounters?

And if any of that was true, what was he going to do about it?

CHAPTER THREE

AUTUMN WASN'T ENTIRELY sure how it happened. But after dinner and a glass of Cognac, somehow she and Jack announced they were leaving at the same time.

Ivy grinned. "That's great! This way Jack can give you a lift home."

"I'm in Queens," Autumn quickly reminded her. "That's too far. I can take the subway."

"Nonsense," Sebastian said, handing Autumn her black wool coat. "It's not like Jack has anywhere else to go."

Jack smiled stiffly.

And how could Autumn blame him? She hadn't exactly taken *every* jab at him she could, but she'd used more than one of the opportunities presented to remind him he was pond scum.

Watching him try to get them out of this one would be her last mean thing. She swore. On the day of the wedding, she would be nothing but sweet to him. Or at least sort of friendly.

He caught her gaze, and she lifted her chin in challenge. *Go ahead, rich kid. Get us out of this.*

His blue eyes flickered with something that looked like humor and her resolve shook. *Had he gone from squirming to enjoying this? How could he possibly enjoy this?*

"You know what? I'm happy to give Autumn a ride home."

Her eyes bugged. He wasn't enjoying this! He was turning everything back on her!

"That's not necessary."

He smiled at her. "Of course, it is. I'm not totally familiar with the route, but don't you have to take a bus to get to a subway stop?"

"I can get a ride share."

"Don't be ridiculous. What kind of a gentleman would I be to let a lady go through all that this late at night?"

"One who knows that the lady is perfectly capable of getting herself home."

"Of course, she is," Jack said, motioning for her to walk to the door. "But a gentleman still enjoys doing a kindness."

Ivy laughed as he kissed her cheek when he said goodbye. "Such a smooth talker."

Sebastian slapped his back, then hugged Autumn before she stepped out of the townhouse.

"I'll see you on Monday," Ivy called, waving goodbye.

Then the townhouse door closed.

Autumn turned on Jack. "I am not letting you drive me home!"

Jack talked through a big smile he had pasted on his face. "You better. Sebastian and Ivy are at the window, watching us."

"Damn it!"

He waved off his driver before he could open the limo door and handled it himself, directing Autumn to get inside. "Is that any way for a lady to talk?"

"What do you care if I'm a lady or not?" She turned back to look at the window. The drapes had closed. She was free. She sidestepped Jack. "They're gone. I'll see myself home."

"Wait!"

She ignored Jack's call and headed up the street, pulling her phone from her pocket so she could call a ride share.

The sound of tires crunched beside her. Through her peripheral vision she saw the limo inching along the curb next to her.

The back window lowered. Jack said, "Come on. Get in. Let us take you home."

"I already ordered a ride share."

"Seriously," Jack said as the limo crawled along. "It is no problem for me to give you a ride."

"Maybe it's a problem for me?"

"Really?"

"Maybe I don't want to spend thirty minutes in a car with you trying to figure out what to say. I don't like you. You dumped me. Our spending time together is the definition of awkward."

He said nothing.

Ah. He agreed.

"At least let me wait for your ride share."

"It's a free country, but you look like you're stalking me driving up beside me like that."

"Okay, here's the thing. I know you're mad that I left after our night together and didn't call. But there were extenuating circumstances."

The limo continued to inch along beside her and she sighed. "Don't be so smug, thinking I'm still mad after five years. I'm a mature adult. Sometimes things just aren't what they seem. I have moved on."

"You'd never prove it by me."

"Hey, just because I got past what happened doesn't mean I want to be friends with you."

He winced.

"I'm serious. You played me for a fool."

"What if I told you that had it not been for the extenuating circumstances, I would not have played you for a fool."

Something hopeful rippled through her and she cursed it. Seriously? She could not give him a pass, have fun with him at the wedding then have him drop out of her life again. "What might have happened doesn't matter. What does matter is that you're a scoundrel. An oaf."

"An *oaf*? No one says *oaf* anymore."

She glanced at her phone. "Hey, my ride's around the corner. He must have just dropped someone off."

She stepped back so she could peer down the street to see when the car turned. Within seconds the blue sedan was driving toward her.

She waved her arm and the car eased to the curb. She fake-smiled at Jack. "See you at the wedding."

She got into the car and they sped off, leaving Jack's limo in the dust. Grateful she didn't have to see him until the rehearsal dinner, she leaned back on the seat, and relaxed for the first two minutes. But then her phone buzzed with a message. She glanced down. It was from Ivy.

Hey everyone!
I was thinking about our introduction dances for the reception, and I decided we needed something more special than a plain announcement of your names as you enter the dance floor. So, I've decided that each couple will have a "piece" of a bigger dance routine to be performed by the entire bridal party. I've hired a dance instructor to do the choreography and he'll also teach each couple the routine. Because everyone's part is

different, there's no need to practice together. Each couple only need to learn their segment of the routine! We think it will only take three sessions.

Isn't this fun? Greg will text your practice times. I've given him all of your numbers.

Autumn groaned. She didn't want to be with Jack at all. But three "sessions" learning a dance routine? Being in his arms? Swaying up against each other?

That was one step too far!

If she didn't know better, she'd think Ivy either knew about their one-night stand or suspected something.

But how could she? No one knew. At least Autumn didn't think so.

She swung around in the back of the sedan, spotting Jack's limo behind them before it turned right and disappeared.

Could *he* have told Sebastian?

She groaned. After the way he pretended they didn't know each other when they saw one another that morning, forcing her to follow his lead, she would clobber him if he had!

Jack showed up at the dance studio Monday evening at six. Sunday morning, he'd called Sebastian and as smoothly as possible tried to get himself and Autumn out of this. But happy Sebastian seemed oblivious to Jack's maneuvering.

Sunday afternoon, he'd received a text from the dance instructor with the times of his practices with Autumn. So here he was. He removed his suit jacket and tie, hanging them on a hook near the door and rolled the sleeves of his white shirt to the elbows. He still wore his loafers from work that day, but he decided that was fine. At the wedding, he'd be dancing in a tux and good shoes. His current clothes were close to that. It would be good practice.

Autumn, however, would be dancing in a gown.

He sniffed a laugh. Wonder how she planned to accommodate that?

Not that he'd been thinking about her. At least not too much. And he wasn't thinking about her as much as working to figure out a way that being with her for the entire day of the wedding wouldn't be too awkward.

He'd apologized. He'd told her as much of his story as he was comfortable sharing. He wasn't sure what else to do.

After introducing himself to the dance instructor, Greg, an average-sized, average-looking guy in jeans and a T-shirt, who beamed with happiness, Jack edged over to the balance barre and glanced at his phone. Autumn was two minutes late.

Hope built that she'd talked Ivy out of this idea, but then the glass door of the studio opened, and Autumn blew in with a gust of wind. Snowflakes frosted her hair. Laughing, she brushed them off. Then she saw him and deflated.

His chest tightened. All these years, if he ever thought of Autumn at all it was to consider her the first in his string of bad luck with women. Now that he'd begun seeing things from her perspective, he felt like a crumb, a snake, someone who owed *her*.

"I couldn't talk Sebastian out of this," he said as she approached him.

"I couldn't talk Ivy out of it either."

The normal tone of her voice encouraged him. "At least we agree about something."

She sniffed and removed her wool coat, revealing black yoga pants and a pink T-shirt that outlined her curves. He remembered those curves warm and silky beneath his palms and took a quick breath to dispel the memory.

"Sorry about the yoga pants. I keep them in my office for when I work late." She glanced down at them, then up at Jack. "I should have practiced in my dress. At least that's somewhat like a gown."

"You look…" *Really hot.* Hot enough that his chest tightened and spectacular memories of their night together cascaded through his brain again. "Fine."

She tossed her coat on an available hook and sat on the bench against the wall to remove her clunky boots. Then she rummaged through her huge purse and pulled out...

"Are those ballet slippers?" He caught her gaze. "You took ballet?"

"A very acceptable thing for girls to do when I was growing up."

He frowned.

"What? You think because I'm clumsy I couldn't possibly dance?"

She was not clumsy. Especially not in bed. She was smooth and graceful.

"No. I was wondering what purpose it serves to learn our part in ballet slippers when you'll be wearing wedding shoes when we actually dance."

She rose. "Not if I slip into these under the table before we're introduced."

He laughed, remembering why he'd liked her so much the night he'd met her. Her blissful pragmatism.

Greg ambled over. Glancing at Jack, he said, "This is your partner for the wedding?"

He and Autumn simultaneously said, "Yes."

Autumn added, "I'm Autumn."

Happy Greg grinned. "Then let's get started." He walked to the opposite side of the room and motioned for Autumn and Jack to stay where they were. "Your dance begins with a series of twirls that gets you to the center of the floor."

Jack balked. "I'm twirling?"

"No. You twirl your partner."

He relaxed. "Thank God."

Autumn giggled. "What? Twirling is a threat to your masculinity?"

"No. I don't want to look like a fool. There'll be lots of important people at that wedding. Most of them eat at my restaurants. I don't want to look like the guy who can't twirl."

"*You're* the one worried about being clumsy?"

"Hey, I didn't laugh at you when you insinuated you were clumsy." He hadn't laughed because he'd remembered her in bed. Definitely not clumsy.

"Oh, poor baby."

Another memory shot through him. The night they'd stayed together, he'd complained about a meeting the following afternoon and she'd walked her fingers up his chest and said, "Oh, poor baby," before she'd completely annihilated him with a kiss.

He sucked in a breath. He had to stop thinking about that night.

"Take your partner's hand and raise her arm enough that you can twirl her out to the floor. I'm guessing it will be three or four twirls before you get to the center of the dance area."

Jack did as he was told. He wasn't completely clueless. He'd actually learned the basics of dancing in lessons his mom had insisted on when he was fourteen because she believed a polished gentleman should be able to dance. He'd groaned and argued, but once he'd begun going to charity events, he'd realized how smart of a decision that had been.

He raised Autumn's arm and twirled her three times, mesmerized by the way she sprang to her toes and made the simple movement of twirling look majestic and elegant.

Her ability gave him confidence and they did two more twirls to get to the center.

"Lovely." Greg smiled at Autumn. "You've taken lessons."

"Only every Saturday morning for what seemed like an eternity."

He laughed.

Jealousy crept up on Jack, but he stopped it because it was wrong. There'd never be anything between him and Autumn. She disliked him and three failed engagements was enough to make any man take a step back and evaluate. He clearly wasn't relationship material.

Greg walked over and positioned them. "When you come out of the twirl, I want you to stand like this." He motioned for Jack to stay where he was and turned Autumn to face Jack.

"Now," Greg continued. "I want you both to shift right, then left, as if you're trying to see over each other's shoulder—"

Jack grimaced. "What kind of dance is this?"

"It's free style. Ivy wants us to tell the story of her relationship with Sebastian. Apparently, she and Sebastian were at odds when they first met and had to grow to love each other. Because you two are the first couple, you'll be demonstrating that discord."

Autumn said, "Should be a piece of cake for us to demonstrate discord."

Jack sniffed a laugh.

Greg smiled. "Well, those movements are only about two seconds of your dance. Lean left, lean right, get into the waltz position. Then it's a waltz around the floor until you are beside Ivy and Sebastian where you will stop, and the next couple will be introduced."

"Okay." Waltz? He loved to waltz. "Sounds easy."

Greg faced Autumn. "Agree?"

"Absolutely."

Greg clapped. "Then let's start at the beginning. Twirl, twirl, twirl. Lean left. Lean right. Waltz hold. Then a waltz around the dance floor."

CHAPTER FOUR

AUTUMN AND JACK returned to the side of the room. He took her hand and twirled her to the center of the dance floor, where they stopped and faced each other before they leaned left and right. Then he stepped toward her to get into the waltz hold.

His hand sliding across her back almost made her stumble, but her trusty ballet shoes saved her. Still, that didn't stop the warmth that spread up her spine causing tingles of awareness that spawned a million memories. Mostly of how they'd laughed at the gala where they'd met. He'd snagged champagne for her from passing waiters and bribed one of them to always have a glass of whiskey on his tray. By the end of the night, they were both tipsy. And happy. They'd seemed like two peas in a pod. Especially when they'd danced.

She put her hand on his shoulder and the memories multiplied. She could almost feel them gliding along the floor, gazing into each other's eyes as if they couldn't believe their luck in finding each other. But more than that, she knew what he felt like beneath that shirt. She could picture his muscled shoulders, back and chest.

She swallowed.

"You okay?"

She raised her eyes to meet his gaze. Those stunning blue eyes almost did her in. She glanced away, saying, "Yes. Fine."

Jack took the first step to lead her in the waltz. His feet were sure. His movements balanced.

Greg clapped. "Stop! Stop! Stop!" He ambled over. "Seriously? You had hundreds of dance lessons, but you don't know you're to look your partner in the eye?"

Autumn stepped out of the hold. "Yes. I'm sorry. I'm just a little scattered today."

Jack's head tilted as he studied her.

"Long day at work," she qualified.

Greg sighed. "It doesn't take a lot of energy to look in your partner's eyes."

She took a breath. "I know."

"Good. Then let's start from the top."

She and Jack walked back to the side of the room. Greg said, "Go."

Jack took her hand and twirled her four times to get her to the center of the dance floor. They leaned left, then right. He stepped toward her and joined their hands as he slid his other arm around her waist.

Her palm tingling, she placed her fingers on his shoulder, then raised her eyes to meet his gaze.

The world upended. Memories of dancing together at the gala whispered through her, then making love. They'd been as close as two people could be and now they were pretending not to know each other.

He effortlessly waltzed them in a circle around the dance floor. But with her gaze connected to his, everything inside her shivered. Not merely with remembered sensations. But with the feeling of rejection. With the sense that she wasn't good enough. The sense that—just as her dad always said—she was average, made to be a worker bee. That she should keep her head down and do her job and hopefully find a man who could take care of her.

The thoughts penetrated so deep, she faltered, tripping as she was gazing into the eyes of the man she'd thought she could fall in love with.

Jack covered her misstep and effortlessly got them to their stopping place. Yanking her gaze from his, she jerked out of his arms.

Greg said, "That was lovely. Jack, you waltz like a dream. You have nothing to be afraid of." He turned to Autumn. "Since you'll be wearing a gown. No one will even notice if you bobble a step."

I will.

Jack will.

And he already thinks there's something wrong with me. A reason not to ever call again. A reason to never see me again.

She did not want to be unbalanced or foolish in his arms.

Damn it. She was not what her father thought. She did not want Jack to think she was. She would not trip in his arms again.

She took a cleansing breath and pasted on a smile for Greg. "Thank you. That was fun and honestly I think we have the hang of it."

Jack continued to study her.

Greg glanced at his phone. "Second couple will be here in five minutes. Do you want to go over it one more time or do you think you have it?"

"We're fine," Autumn quickly said, then smiled to take the sting out of it. "I'm tired. I had that bad day, remember?" She smiled again.

"Honestly, you two have the easiest of the dances," Greg said. "One more run through on Wednesday and you should be solid."

"Sounds great," Autumn agreed as she headed for her coat and clunky boots. She slid them on and walked to the door. "I'll see you on Wednesday night."

"See you then," Greg replied, but Jack said nothing.

Which was fine. They had one more dance

lesson, the rehearsal dinner and one wedding to get through, then they'd never see each other again. She might be in the same job she'd been in five years ago, but she was extremely good at it. The current CEO was getting up in years and would eventually retire and she would step into his shoes.

That was her plan.

She was not less than. She was a smart woman, gifted in fundraising. With a plan. A good, solid plan to move into the job she was born to do.

One guy who dumped her and one misstep on the dance floor changed nothing.

Tuesday morning, Autumn got a call from Ivy, who bubbled over with excited questions. Making a cup of coffee, Autumn told the bride-to-be that the dance lesson had been fine.

"That's all? Just fine?"

"It's a very simple dance," Autumn said, smiling in the hope the positivity of it would translate to her voice.

"Maybe too simple?"

"No. It's lovely. I love to waltz and Jack's a great dancer. In fact, we did so well last night Greg thinks we only need one more lesson."

After a few seconds of silence, Ivy said, "Jack didn't say anything offensive, did he?"

Autumn laughed. "As we were both focused on learning a dance?"

"Jack can be chatty."

"Does he typically say offensive things when he's chatty?"

"No." Ivy's voice turned petulant. "It's just that I thought you'd enjoy the lessons."

"Dancing was fun," Autumn said, scrambling for something positive to say. Everything about the wedding was important to Ivy. She wanted everyone to love every step of the process as much as she did. And Autumn loved how happy Ivy was and wanted to keep her that way. "The dance is going to be really cool. I think it will be entertaining for the guests."

"Good. Great. You'll all have fun and it will be brilliant. I am glad I thought of it and I'm glad you like it."

Autumn frowned. Ivy was babbling and she never babbled. "Is everything okay with the wedding?"

"Yes! Wonderful. Meeting with the florist again today."

"Oh, that's fun."

"Yes. It really is."

But Ivy had that strange tone in her voice again. Still, she didn't probe any deeper about the dance lesson with Jack, so when she said goodbye Autumn went back to dressing for work.

As she walked out the door, a weird sensation spiraled through her and she stopped on the little porch of her second-floor apartment. She'd told Ivy she didn't think she and Jack needed the final two lessons—

Then Ivy had changed the subject even though she'd been asking questions—

Was Autumn crazy to notice that or did that mean something?

She shook her head with a laugh. She was monitoring the bride for signs of nerves, but that subject change had been meaningless.

She hoped.

Because when Ivy had a bee in her bonnet about something she wouldn't rest until she resolved it.

Jack stepped out of the elevator into the reception area for the corporate offices of Step Inside when his phone rang. Seeing the caller was Sebastian, he said, "What's up?"

"I have a favor to ask."

"Anything for the groom to be."

"We're cake tasting this afternoon."

Jack grimaced at his friend's plight. "I thought you'd chosen a cake."

"We thought we had too. Thing is… Ivy's decided everyone should get their own tiny wedding cake to take home and she wants everybody to have a choice of flavor. She's going for goofy things. New flavors designed by the baker. I'm sort of campaigning for just plain chocolate cake."

"Your favorite."

"Is that so wrong?"

Jack laughed.

"We've already chosen four, but up to this point, chocolate never made the grade. This afternoon at the bakery, I want you to help me get chocolate into the rotation."

Jack laughed at the way he said rotation as if the cake was vying to be a starting pitcher for the Yankees, then he realized what Sebastian had said. "You want me to taste cakes?"

"Yes. As a former chef, your opinion holds weight. If you come prepared to taste the chocolate and say it's the best thing ever created, Ivy will listen."

It was a bit odd. But he'd seen how stressful the wedding plans had become, so Jack could be a good sport and help out his friend. "Okay. I'll be there." He stepped into his office. Furnished in an ultra-modern minimalist style, with a pale wood desk and a buttery brown leather for the chair, the clean lines of both the room and the furnishings forced him to keep his big, shiny desk empty. He walked over to the hidden closet where he stored his coat. "Text me the address."

"Okay. Three o'clock. I'll see you then."

"Right. See you at three."

Turning away from the closet, he stopped as a weird sensation washed through him. He hadn't thought about being a chef in years. When his mom ran Step Inside, he'd been the head chef of their flagship restaurant. That was where he'd created the menu that had made them so successful that they could put restaurants in the five boroughs and expand into New Jersey. Before she'd died, they'd been discussing creating a research and development kitchen where he could create and test recipes to come up with dishes that would rotate, keeping their menu original and innovative.

He shook his head to clear it. That had been the culmination of their dream. His mom running the business end and him creating. But when she died, he'd taken over the business and found a way to update the menu by subcontracting chefs like Randolph to create new meals. It was that decision that solidified his ability to take over the business with the board his mother had chosen.

It was that decision that had made him who he was today. One hell of a businessman.

So why did it feel so odd suddenly? Like Sebastian mentioning he'd been a chef had dragged him further back in time than seeing Autumn had—

Actually, he could probably blame these new feelings on seeing Autumn, too.

That night had changed so much about his life. He stopped being a son, stopped being a chef, literally lost his entire family and had to pick up the ball and finish the game for his mother.

But it had worked and worked well. He wouldn't question it or analyze choices that had succeeded.

With a ton of emails in his inbox, he dismissed his thoughts and spent an hour reading before he met with the company's chief financial officer and his team who would handle crafting the financials for the new five-year plan.

At one o'clock, he had lunch at one of his own restaurants. He'd changed from his suit into jeans and a sweater with a black leather jacket. No one recognized him, so it gave him the perfect opportunity to observe.

And maybe to be a little bit proud that he'd brought his mother's vision to glorious life.

But on the heels of that pride came the sorrow and the longing to have watched *her* live her dream. He recognized that Sebastian's throwaway comment had spawned memories of the years of dedication it had taken to turn Step Inside into something remarkable. But it felt wrong to be proud of himself. Wrong to enjoy the success.

So, he'd forget all that, forget Autumn, forget Sebastian's throwaway comment and focus on the wedding. When his driver arrived with his limo, he texted the address Sebastian had given him to his driver and settled into the backseat, reading emails on his phone during the ride to the cake tasting. Twenty minutes later, the limo pulled up at a townhouse.

"This is it?"

Arnie, his driver, turned around on his seat. "This is the address."

"Stay close a minute while I make sure Sebastian didn't transpose a number or something."

He got out of the limo, walked up to the townhouse door and rang the bell. Sebastian answered. "Come in. We're all in the kitchen."

He waved to Arnie and headed inside. "This is a house."

"The home of the baker Ivy chose to make our cakes."

Sebastian led him down a hall replete with antiques and Oriental rugs. They walked into an open kitchen with stunning white cabinets, quartz counter tops and tall-backed stools around the biggest island Jack had ever seen.

It was also very similar to what he and his mom had planned for his test kitchen. The memory of meeting with the architect and even approving plans rippled through him.

"Here he is now," Ivy said, racing over to kiss Jack's cheek. "I can't wait for you to test the strawberry cream filled."

He shoved the unwanted memories to the back of his mind and returned Ivy's check kiss. "Meaning, you're on team strawberry?"

"Yes. We have one slot to fill. I adore the strawberry. Sebastian likes the chocolate. And Autumn is team lemon."

He saw her then. Sitting on one of the tall-backed stools at the island, she had five or six pieces of cake in front of her. But her hair hung straight, almost to her shoulders and she wore a slim red dress that came to her knees and high-high heels that he was positive would make her look tall and sexy.

"Autumn."

She glanced at him. "Jack."

Even after three times seeing each other there was still something off in the way they treated each other. He'd thought dancing together had melted some of the ice between them, but she'd gotten odd at the end of the session and raced away so quickly he hadn't even heard her say goodbye.

Anybody who wasn't wrapped up in wedding preparations would realize they barely tolerated each other—

Or maybe somebody who *was* wrapped up in wedding preparations had noticed. And maybe that's why Ivy kept throwing them together.

Ivy slid her hand beneath his arm and led him to the spot right beside Autumn.

Yeah. She'd noticed.

"Here's your cake set up." The happy bride pointed at the plate holding the yellow slice and said, "That's the lemon."

She then pointed at the pink "strawberry cream," then at two nondescript versions with names like "tangerine torte" and "special birthday," and finally she pointed at the chocolate. "And that, of course, is Sebastian's pick."

Jack said, "Yum. I'm a big fan of chocolate."

Ivy snorted. "You're a friend of the guy who likes chocolate. You don't get to make your choice until you've tasted all of them."

He winced. "Even that special birthday thing that looks like the color of a zombie?"

Autumn laughed unexpectedly and his gaze jumped to her.

"I knew it reminded me of something. I just couldn't figure out what it was."

Jack's lips lifted into a hopeful smile. Maybe some of the ice had melted after all?

The baker sighed. "It's a theme color." Older, stout and dressed in a traditional chef's uniform of white coat and toque blanche, he gave Jack a you-should-know-that look as he ambled over to the island. "It was created for the birthday party of Angelina Montgomery last year. Guests couldn't get enough of it."

"Oh, yes, Mark! I remember!" Ivy said. "Guests gushed about that cake for months."

Mark took a breath, lifting his nose in the air as if he were looking down on them. "They're still gushing."

Autumn pressed her lips together to keep from laughing and caught Jack's gaze again. He was totally with her. He understood the pride of the great chefs and bakers. He'd been proud of every damned thing he'd created. But sometimes the pretense was just a little bit funny.

He rolled his eyes and Autumn nodded. They were absolutely on the same page.

Memories of the click he'd felt with her five years ago poured through him. He hadn't been born into this life the way Ivy had. Neither had Autumn. Both had worked to get here and worked even harder to belong here. But they'd both also hung on to their normal lives, their normal values.

Ivy turned to Jack. "Jack, this is Mark Patel. His cakes are divine."

Jack offered his hand across the big island. "It's a pleasure to meet you."

Stretching forward, the baker took Jack's hand to shake. "A pleasure to meet you too."

Autumn slid one of Jack's slices closer to him. "Try the zombie one. It's actually pretty good."

Mark nodded approvingly. "I accomplish that gray color with blueberry juice which also gives the cake just a bit of a tangy flavor."

"That had been what I thought," Jack said as he took the seat beside Autumn and picked up the fork. He cut a bite of the cake and ate it. Flavor burst on his tongue.

"Oh, that *is* good."

The baker stuck his nose in the air again. "Of course, it is."

"But, Jack," Sebastian reminded him. "You like chocolate."

"I do," Jack agreed, sliding the zombie cake away and reaching for the chocolate. He took a bite. "Oh, my God." He jerked his gaze to the baker. "Are you kidding me? This is the best cake I've ever eaten."

Sebastian leaned in and whispered, "Don't over sell it."

"I'm not overselling." He caught Mark's gaze again. "This is amazing."

"And Jack knows amazing," Sebastian said, glancing over at Mark. "He owns Step Inside."

Mark's expression said he was impressed. "I've eaten there. And also heard good things from your chefs."

Autumn said, "You *own* Step Inside?"

He winced, expecting some sort of wise crack. The ice might be thawing but it hadn't melted completely. "Yes."

"I love those restaurants."

Pride rolled through him. He tried to stop it. After all, he was only following his mother's plans. But it bubbled up. He swore he could feel his chest swelling.

"And I like the chocolate too."

Autumn's voice filled the sudden void in the kitchen.

Surprised that Autumn had sided with him on the chocolate cake, Jack peeked over at her. The click of rightness they'd shared the night they'd spent together tiptoed back. Too busy having fun, they hadn't shared facts of their lives until she'd told him a bit about her job when they were lying in bed together.

But that night, the past hadn't mattered. Only the present had. The connection they'd felt. The fun they'd had being themselves.

Jack was glad when Ivy broke the spell by groaning and Sebastian laughed. "It looks like I get chocolate after all."

Ivy sighed dramatically. "All right. You win. Chocolate it is."

With the decision made, Mark nudged the plates closer to his guests. "Eat! These cakes are too good to throw away."

Steeped in conflicting emotions, Jack quietly said, "You could donate them to homeless shelters."

Mark batted a hand. "Everything but the pieces

on the plates can definitely go to the shelters. Pieces on the plates must be eaten." He grinned. "Can I get anyone a glass of wine?"

Sebastian said, "I'd love one."

Ivy agreed. "Me too. Though I'm only eating one piece of cake because I have a wedding gown to fit into."

Autumn seconded that. "I have a dress to fit into, too. I also have a long trip home." She rose from her stool. "So, if you don't mind, I'll be leaving."

Mark jumped into action, scooping up the plate with her slice of lemon cake that had only one bite taken out. "Let me box this up for you." He grinned. "For breakfast tomorrow."

Autumn glanced at the cake with longing in her eyes. "It would make a great breakfast."

Jack almost told her she was perfect just the way she was. She didn't need to diet. She had curves in all the right places. But not only was this the wrong place and time, the urge itself confused him. She didn't like him. He didn't do relationships. There was no reason for them to get personal. All he needed was for the ice to thaw a little more. He didn't even want to be her friend. After this wedding they'd go their separate ways.

"It will make a fabulous breakfast!" Mark slid the cake into a handy takeout container. Obviously, this wasn't the first cake tasting in his house.

Autumn happily took it. "Thank you."

Mark said, "You're welcome."

She turned to Ivy. "If you need me, call."

"Okay."

Then she waved to Sebastian before she left the kitchen, cake in hand, and slipped out the front door.

Jack blinked, surprised at how quickly she was gone and even more surprised no one had asked him to give Autumn a ride home. Then he remembered the cold war feeling he'd sensed he and Autumn were throwing off when he first arrived.

They might have warmed up over her love of his restaurants, the proud baker and the chocolate cake, but she'd barely acknowledged him when she left.

No. She hadn't acknowledged him at all.

She'd thanked Mark, told Ivy to call if she needed anything and waved to Sebastian.

And nothing to him.

He waited for Ivy to say something about Autumn. Maybe to call him out over the way they barely spoke to each other. She didn't. He expected Sebastian to say something twenty minutes later when he walked Jack to the door. He didn't. He simply said a happy goodbye.

Jack walked down the sidewalk to his limo

with the godawful feeling that it wasn't other people who didn't like the cold war between him and Autumn. It was *him*.

He'd hurt her. Good excuse or not, he'd hurt her.

And if he wanted the two of them to get along for this wedding, he was going to have to tell her why.

CHAPTER FIVE

AUTUMN STOPPED AT the door of the dance studio and took a long breath. Fat white snowflakes fell to the sidewalk, making the city a winter wonderland and covering the hood of her down jacket. But she needed a minute to remind herself she was a strong woman who refused to be attracted to a man who was probably a player, someone who had lots of one-night stands and countless pretty girls willing to go anywhere he wanted any time he wanted. The man *owned* Step Inside. One of the best restaurants she'd ever eaten at.

He was way out of her league.

Unfortunately, he hadn't behaved like a rich guy at the cake testing. In fact, he'd been the Jack she'd met at the summer gala five years before. He'd made her laugh at least twice. And, God help her, now that she knew he owned Step Inside, she *did* understand how busy and demanding his life had probably been for the past few years.

She couldn't remember him mentioning what he did for a living the night they'd met at the gala.

They'd been preoccupied gazing into each other's eyes and having fun. But now that he'd told her he managed a string of highly successful restaurants, the problem was clear.

Of course, she liked him. He was gorgeous, funny, rich.

But she was Autumn Jones. Average at best. Not the girl Prince Charming would choose to dance with at the ball—unless there was no one else around. Historically, young singles were at a premium at a gala planned to entice wealthy people to donate money.

She hadn't been a choice that night. She'd been the only option.

Which was why she needed the minute to regroup. If she continued to think back to the gala and remember how attuned they seemed to be, she could forget that they weren't two peas in a pod. Plus, she wasn't the same woman she was when she had met him. She might have always wanted to be CEO of Raise Your Voice, but now that goal was in reach. Gerry was old enough that he would soon be retiring.

She couldn't afford a misstep. She couldn't afford to become so involved with a man that she'd end up part of his life rather than having her own life. She'd seen enough of that with her parents. Her mom waited on her dad hand and foot and threw herself into making sure her kids had good lives, but she didn't seem to have a life of her own. Autumn wanted a career. She wanted to help hundreds of people achieve their goals. She didn't have time for a man or a family.

Her resolve to keep her distance restored, she entered the dance studio.

Unlike their first lesson, Jack wasn't yet there.

She couldn't breathe a sigh of relief that she wouldn't see him that night. Even if he wasn't available for a lesson, they'd have to make it up. She wanted to get this final session over with. She didn't want any more confusing encounters. Didn't want to understand him anymore. Didn't want to see peeks of the guy she'd met at the Raise Your Voice gala. She just wanted them to do their part for the wedding and never see each other again.

She took off her coat and sat on the bench to put on her ballet slippers. The door opened and Jack walked in. "Cold out there."

"And lots of snow," Greg agreed, ambling into the studio from a door in the back. "I hope you have a dependable way home."

Before Jack could say anything, Autumn said, "I usually stay with Ivy and Sebastian when it snows this much."

Jack said, "There's no need. I can take you."

Now that she had a solid understanding of what had happened between them, she ventured a smile. "Ivy wants to go over some things about the wedding." Thank God. She and Jack might be getting along but that didn't mean she wanted to spend almost an hour in a car with him, trying to think of things to talk about without getting too chummy, causing her to remember how very much she'd liked him that night.

"And speaking of Ivy," Greg said. "She's changed your dance a bit."

Jack groaned. He removed his overcoat and walked it to the row of hooks on the wall by the big window, revealing a dark suit. After he took off his jacket, he turned to face Greg and Autumn's heart fluttered. He looked amazing in the dark trousers and white shirt. He rolled the sleeves to his elbows then took off his tie and he looked even better. Professional sexy.

Walking to Greg, he said, "I liked what we had."

"You pulled off the waltz like a pro—"

"Because I had about six lessons as a kid and learning to waltz took up most of them."

Greg batted a hand. "You'll get this too. Especially since the new version isn't much more difficult. We're going to add the basic Charleston step right after the look left, look right move."

Her shoes on, Autumn rose from the bench. Greg reached for her hand and guided her onto the dance floor. "So, you're going to look left, then look right," he said as he reminded her of the move that she and Jack already knew. "Then you do a twirling pivot that puts you beside Jack."

He demonstrated the step so that he stood beside Autumn. "Then you do the basic Charleston step. Take a step back with the right foot. Then swing the left leg back in a kicking motion. Bring the left foot forward again and return to the starting position. Then, with the right foot loose, kick it forward. Bring it back. Blah. Blah. Blah. We're going to repeat that step five times. Meaning the left foot gets five kicks and so does the right."

Jack stared at him.

Autumn pressed her lips together to keep from laughing. It was fun to find something he wasn't good at. Though with the way he waltzed, he'd probably get this easily.

Greg smiled encouragingly. "It's really a very simple dance once you master the primary step."

Looking like a deer in the headlights, Jack said, "But I'll be in front of people. Every additional step adds to the potential embarrassment."

"Why don't we try learning the move, before we ease it into the routine?" Autumn asked, taking pity on him. "Plus, I know the Charleston. Just follow my lead."

Greg glanced at Jack. Autumn smiled hopefully. Jack took a breath.

"Okay. Yeah. Sure. But Ivy does realize this

could backfire, right? Any one of us could go on that dance floor and make a fool of ourselves."

"And you know what?" Greg said supportively. "The guests will love it. They will love that you tried. Everyone roots for an underdog."

Autumn motioned for Jack to stand beside her on the dance floor.

He approached, mumbling, "I do not want to be the underdog."

She held back a snort as he lined up beside her. Now that she knew who he was it was easy to see his objections as funny. He could end up on the wrong side of a society page critic's article.

Greg said, "All right. Let's have a go at this. Take a step back on the right leg. Swing the left leg back in a kicking motion. Bring the left foot forward again and return to the starting position. Then with the right foot loose, kick it forward. Bring it back."

Autumn put her hand on Jack's forearm to stop him. "Forget the words. Watch my feet."

He frowned. She motioned for him to look at her feet before she brought her right leg back, then her left, then kicked it forward.

He brought his right leg back, then his left, then kicked it forward.

"I feel stupid kicking."

"Pretend you're playing for the Giants. You've got the center holding the football up for you and you're going to kick it through the uprights."

One of his eyebrows rose.

"I'm serious. You might not want to kick your leg as high as the kicker on a football team does. But it's the same basic concept. It's also a little more manly that way. Something you can sink your teeth into."

She repeated the step and he followed until they were able to string five of them together.

When they were done, Greg clapped. "Very nice. Now, let's try the thing from the top. Go back to the side. Twirl onto the dance floor. Look left, look right. Charleston step five times. Waltz hold. Waltz."

They walked to the side of the dance floor but before he gave them the signal to start, Greg added music. The song began with a gentle gathering of notes that made it easy for Jack to twirl her to the dance floor, then the music changed subtly for the look left, look right, then it shifted again for the Charleston steps, which Jack bungled.

He sighed. She smiled at him and said, "Let's just go over it one more time."

"Yeah. And are we going to go over it at the wedding before we do the dance?"

She shrugged. "If it will help, we can find a private room and go over the whole routine after dinner, before the dance, so it's fresh in your mind."

He ran his hand along the back of his neck. "Actually, that probably would help."

"Then that's what we'll do."

They walked back to the side of the dance floor and Greg restarted the music, but he stopped it again. "What do you say we run through the entire dance. No matter how poorly you think you've done, Jack, I want you to push through it."

Jack took a breath. "You know why he said that, don't you?"

Autumn peered up at him. "To show us that the dance works?"

"No, he wants me to get practice screwing up and soldiering on. So, when I screw up at the wedding, I'll just keep going."

She laughed.

Greg hit the music and Jack twirled Autumn onto the dance floor. They looked left then right, then she did the Charleston step and he followed as best he could. Then they got into the waltz hold and began to dance.

He relaxed completely. This was the part he knew.

"Look how well you're doing."

"This is the dance I took lessons for, remember?"

She held back a wince. "You did okay on the Charleston steps."

"Not really. But thanks."

The waltz ended and they headed back to the

edge of the dance floor. Greg turned on the music and they started the routine from the top.

This time, maybe because the Charleston steps went a little smoother, when Jack took Autumn into his arms for the waltz and looked into her eyes, he felt like he had gone back in time to their night at the gala. His comfort with the waltz meshed with how comfortable he'd been with her five years ago and emotions tumbled around him. He remembered thinking how logical it was for them to go back to her apartment and make love because everything between them was so effortless—

He wasn't the only one who had felt it. She had too. Which was why he owed her an explanation for why he hadn't called.

What they'd had that night was once-in-a-lifetime perfect. Something he hadn't felt before or since and probably wouldn't ever feel again. Technically, he'd ruined what might have been their chance at permanent happiness.

Or maybe better said, Fate had stolen it and she deserved to know that.

Suddenly the sound of Greg applauding filled the dance studio. "That was beautiful, Jack. You certainly have command of the waltz."

He stepped away from Autumn, but their gazes held. Feelings from the night they met swamped him. The sense of finding something that would change his life.

"You can let go of my hand now."

The spell broken, he released her hand. He might be having feelings from all those years ago, but she wasn't. Not only did he have to remember that, and explain what had happened, but also those resurrected emotions weren't valid anymore. They weren't the same people they had been five years ago. They weren't going to pick up where they left off. Especially since neither of them wanted to.

"One more time, then we're done for the night."

They walked back to the edge of the dance floor. Jack twirled her to the center. They looked left and right, did a clumsy version of the Charleston step and began the waltz. Their gazes connected as he whirled them around the floor, and he felt like he could see the whole way into her soul. She didn't have secrets like he did. She didn't tell lies. She'd had a simple upbringing like his and didn't try to pretend she hadn't. She liked who she was. At least, she had liked who she was the night of the highly successful gala for Raise Your Voice that she'd planned and executed to perfection.

Was it any wonder he'd been so drawn to her?

Once again, it was Greg clapping that brought Jack back to the present. He stepped out of the waltz hold, but let go of her hand slowly. As if bewitched, he couldn't stop staring at her, wondering what would have happened between them if that night had ended differently.

"Jack? Are you with us?"

He shook his head and faced Greg. "I'm sorry. I missed what you said."

"I said you're doing very well."

That would have made him laugh if it wasn't so sad that a couple of steps had him tied up in knots. "We both know I'm not."

Autumn said, "Look at it this way. You ace the twirl. Any fool can look left then right. And you are a master at the waltz. You own this dance—"

"Except for the Charleston steps."

"Which you will get. This is only our first day with those steps."

"Yes. But this is our second session. And it's supposed to be our last."

She frowned. "That's right."

Greg said, "Ivy has paid me to provide as many lessons as you want. Technically, Monday was the last lesson Ivy had scheduled for you, the one we thought you wouldn't need. But that's still five days away from the wedding. That gives you a little too much time to forget everything you learned here…or time enough to have another lesson or two."

He glanced at Autumn. "Do you think we can handle one more lesson?"

"Of course we can."

Her easy acceptance relaxed him, reminding him of what a sweet woman she was, and doubled down on his need to tell her what had happened after their one-night stand.

Greg said, "Okay. Monday it is. Now scoot. I have another couple coming in ten minutes."

She changed into her boots then walked to the hooks on the wall and slipped into her coat and gloves. When he saw Autumn wore mittens he smiled.

His resolve to tell her had never been stronger. She also seemed very receptive.

This was his shot.

They stepped out into the falling snow and she laughed. "You know, come February we're going to be really sick of snow, but the first couple of snowfalls are like magic."

He glanced around. "I remember how I used to wait for snow to go sledding."

"My brothers and I did too."

He hit the button on his key fob to unlock his Mercedes. "You have brothers?"

"Two. Both accountants. Both work on Wall Street."

"Yet you chose a charity?"

"For a couple of really good reasons. First and foremost, I couldn't see myself sitting in an office all day talking numbers."

He laughed. "That does get old quickly."

"Second, I like the idea of using my time to help people." Under the light of a streetlamp, she looked up at him. "What about you?"

"Me?"

"How many brothers and sisters do you have?"

He faltered but realized this was actually a perfect introduction to the conversation they needed to have, though chatting on the street wasn't exactly ideal. "No brothers. No sisters. Only child."

"Oh, that must be fun!"

"Yes and no. Look, let me drive you to Ivy and Sebastian's."

She turned her face up into the snow. "Are you kidding? Miss a chance to walk in the snow?"

He couldn't fault her for that. The wet snow indicated that the temps were around freezing. Warmish for a winter night. And the snow was beautiful.

"Can I walk with you?"

"This is a low crime neighborhood. I'll be fine."

"I know you will. There's just a couple of things we need to talk about."

She headed down the street, starting the four-block walk that would get them to Ivy's townhouse. "You mean like how Ivy and Sebastian keep setting us up for things?"

It wasn't what he wanted to discuss, but now that she mentioned it, they probably should talk about that too.

He hit the button on his key fob to relock his Mercedes and fell in step with her. "I think they noticed we were a little icy to each other."

She laughed. "You think?"

He winced. "All right. I *know*."

She laughed again. The sound echoed around them on the almost empty street. "Maybe we should tell them we met before."

"Maybe." Slowing his steps, he faced her. "Not total disclosure though."

"Oh, God no. If we told Ivy we went home together that night, she'd want every detail."

"Could get embarrassing."

She nudged his shoulder with hers. "Or we could twist it into an opportunity to brag."

Her comment was so unexpected, he burst out laughing. "We were pretty good together."

"Pretty good?" she asked, her pace increasing and her steps getting longer. "We could have done a demo video for YouTube."

He laughed again, his own voice sounding warmer and happier than he could ever remember hearing it. They'd been bold that night. Brazen, really. And so damn happy.

They walked a block in silence. Then she mentioned Christmas shopping she had to do, and he didn't stop her. Didn't try to change the subject. He loved the sound of her voice. He loved the conversation about something so simple, yet so important to someone who had a family.

"My dad is definitely a Christmas sweater guy. I think the new sweater I get him every year is the only update to his winter wardrobe."

"I understand that. I actually have a shopper who keeps my closet full of updated clothes."

She stopped. Looked at him. "Really? You have someone who makes sure you have clothes?"

"Underwear and socks too."

She shook her head and started walking again. "Are you going to come in with me so we can tell Ivy and Sebastian they should cool it?"

"Are we going to tell them we know each other?"

"If you think about it, it's part of the explanation."

"True. So, we say we'd met before at the gala but leave everything else out."

She peeked at him. "The good parts."

"Yeah, no sense making them more focused on us than they already are."

"Or steal the thunder from the wedding."

"I think we'd only steal their thunder if we do the YouTube video."

She chortled and his heart swelled. This was how they were the night of the gala. Easy with each other. Happy.

"You're so fixated on the video that I have to wonder if you aren't looking for a little validation."

"No. I don't need validation. I just think…" He glanced over at her. "Making the video recreating that night might be fun."

Time stopped. Even the snowflakes seemed to hang in midair. He remembered peeling off her pretty gown the night they met. Remembered kisses so hot and deep his blood had crackled. Remembered tucking her beside him when she began to fall asleep.

Finally, he said, "I thought that would make you laugh."

She combed her fingers through her hair. "I should have laughed."

But she hadn't. For the same reason his heart was thrumming now. That night had not been funny. It had been joyful. If she was remembering any of the things he was remembering, laughter would not be her reaction. Her breath might stall. Her pulse might scramble. A whole bundle of wishes that things had been different also might tiptoe into her mind.

Because right now he wasn't laughing either.

CHAPTER SIX

AT IVY AND Sebastian's townhouse, Autumn took a step away from Jack. His comments had brought back more intimate memories of that night and her body tingled with remembered passion even as her heart swelled with the disappointment of the weeks that followed.

Shaking off the feeling, she headed to the steps of the front door. "Are you coming in with me?"

He took a step back. "This might not be the right time to tell them about the night we met."

She stopped.

Yeah. He might be right. How could either one of them talk about meeting at a gala and spending the night together without thinking about all the things his video comment brought back? She'd stumble over her words. She might even flush.

She walked back to him. "Maybe I'll have a private talk with Ivy."

He caught her gaze. Snowflakes fell around him. The night was so silent she could hear her own breathing. "You're sure?"

"Yes. And maybe you could mention it to Sebastian."

"Maybe." He looked away then met her gaze again. "For what it's worth. That was probably the best night of my entire life."

She almost said, *I doubt that*, then noticed how serious he was. The light of a streetlight softened his features. His eyes searched hers.

She couldn't lie to a man whose eyes were so sincere or avoid the question that hung in the air. "Yeah. It ranked pretty high on my best night scale too."

The cold space between them suddenly warmed. They really were coming to terms with this. Making peace with it. Maybe even getting to know each other in a way they hadn't had time to do the night they'd met.

Time stood still again. Neither of them made a move to leave.

And then the oddest thing struck her. It felt like a moment for a first kiss. Romantic snow. Just enough nervousness to amplify the attraction that wouldn't let them alone. And curiosity. Sweet, sweet curiosity if everything she remembered was true. Seconds spun into a minute with them gazing into each other's eyes. Feeling the connection they had the night of the gala. Remembering things probably best left forgotten.

Slowly, regretfully, he took a step back. "I've

got a four-block trek to my Mercedes. So, I'll see you."

"I'll see you." She was *not* disappointed that he hadn't kissed her. That would have only confused things. Made her blood race. Filled her heart with that indescribable something only he seemed to inspire. Caused her to yearn for things that couldn't be.

She knew he was out of her league. And his not wanting a relationship with her had made sense. Still, the best-night-of-his-life comment fluttered through her brain again. The expression in his eyes. The warmth in his voice.

Her resolve weakened. Before he could turn to head to his car, she said, "Monday, right?"

Walking backward up the street, he said, "That's our third lesson."

"We can talk about whether or not we need a fourth."

A solid five feet away from her now, he smiled. "Okay."

"Okay." Before she could do something foolish or say something worse, she raced up the steps to Ivy's townhouse, slipped through the door and walked into the foyer.

Her wishful-thinking soul imagined that Jack stood where he had been, staring at the door.

Her heart warmed again, but she forced herself to remember how excited she'd been the first few days after their night together. Every ring of the phone had her heart racing. But he hadn't called. He hadn't texted. He hadn't emailed. Nothing.

The first week she'd been excited. The second week she'd been nervous, the realization that he probably wasn't going to call following her like a zombie. The third week, she knew he hadn't meant a damned word he'd said.

So, no. She wouldn't let that best-night-of-his-life comment change anything.

Thursday whipped by like a normal day. With Raise Your Voice's Valentine's Day Ball a mere two months away, work had begun to multiply enough that Autumn didn't have time to think about Jack Adams.

And if a wayward thought did slide into her brain, she booted it out, reminding herself that no matter how wistful he sounded, they were wrong for each other.

Friday morning, Raise Your Voice CEO Gerry Harding walked to her desk, tapped his fingers on the rim and said, "How about dinner tonight? I like Becco. It's a casual Italian place. I'll meet you there around…" He pondered that. "Let's say seven."

She blinked. The unexpected invitation threw her. The only thing she and Gerry ever spoke about was work. What could he possibly want to discuss with her for an entire dinner—?

Oh, Lord! Maybe he was retiring?

Her heart sped up. If he was, all those dreams she'd created as a little girl were about to come true. She'd be the boss. And not just of any old company, but a charity that helped people. She'd finally be the person she'd known was inside her all along.

Still, she couldn't panic or look overeager. "Sure. Seven is great and I love Italian food."

He knocked on her desk again. "I'll meet you there. Don't bring your bank card. This is Raise Your Voice business."

"Okay."

He walked away and she took a long, life-sustaining breath. Holy cats. Raise Your Voice business? Could that be anything other than Gerry's retirement?

Oh, dear God, it was happening—

Or at least she thought it was happening. She would not jump the gun. That was another thing Jack ghosting her had taught her. Never, ever, ever make assumptions.

A great debate raged in her head the rest of the day as she worked to figure out anything else Gerry might want to discuss with her other than to tell her he was retiring.

Nothing came.

She stayed at the office until six forty-five and took a ride share to West Forty-Sixth Street.

Gerry was waiting for her inside the door of the restaurant. She hung her black wool coat, and a hostess began leading them through the tables. Halfway there she swore she saw the back of Jack's head.

Which was stupid. Ridiculous. *How could she recognize the back of his head?* Still, curiosity had her gaze swinging around after they'd passed his table and sure enough. It was him.

"'Of all the gin joints...'" Autumn mumbled as she seated herself across from her boss and— damn it!—across from Jack.

Gerry said, "I'm sorry. I missed what you said."

"Old movie quote. From *Casablanca*."

"Great movie," Gerry said, opening his menu. "Are you an old movie buff or a romantic?"

"Old movie buff," she said, refusing to let anyone think she might be romantic. That was another notion Jack ghosting her had squashed.

Her phone pinged with a text. Out of habit, she glanced at it.

Dating grandpas now?

Her head jerked up and her eyes homed in on Jack, who sat smirking at her. She didn't know what he was smirking about. He was single, sitting with two couples.

Gerry peeked over the top of his menu. "Everything okay?"

"Yes. Fine." She smiled again, though her nerve endings jangled.

"Is the text something you need to answer?"

"Actually, it is. It's the kind of text you can't ignore."

He chuckled. "Must be your mom."

Not wanting to lie, she only smiled.

"My wife goes nuts if the kids don't answer a text." He motioned to her phone. "Go ahead."

"Thanks."

The waiter walked up to the table with water and Gerry told him they needed a few minutes to look at the menu.

Autumn typed furiously.

Not able to get a date now? You're the only single in your group.

Across the room, she saw ridiculous Jack shake his head, looking like he was chuckling.

Gerry rose from the table. "I'm going to make a quick trip to wash my hands. You finish your discussion."

Her phone pinged with another text. Gerry left and she grabbed her phone to see Jack's unwanted reply to her text.

This is actually a business meeting.

She snorted.

Aren't you the boss? Shouldn't you be saying something profound? Instead of texting me?

Actually, everybody's talking about their kids now.

Oh.

She knew better than to rib him about that. Some people were sensitive about not having kids. Others didn't want kids and hated being hassled about that choice. That was a landmine she didn't want to step on.

Then a snarky comeback came to her and she laughed to herself as she typed.

Sad that you can't keep control of your own meeting.

Just trying to be a generous, understanding employer.

Damn him. She laughed. When her gaze rose and met his across the room, he smiled at her.

Her heart thrummed. Her nerves sparkled like happy glitter.

Gerry returned. "Everything okay with your mom?"

Though it was better that Gerry thought her mom had texted her, it wasn't true. So, she sidestepped, explaining by saying, "It was just a check-in text."

He snorted. "I've sent that text." He glanced across the table at her. "It usually means you haven't visited in a long time." Without giving her a chance to answer, Gerry picked up the menu. "Any of their dishes are wonderful."

"I love Italian." She put down her menu. "And for the record Sunday is our monthly family dinner. They know I'll be there."

"Oh, that's nice! I should tell my wife about that. We're hit or miss with our kids. It would be good to get on everybody's schedule at least once a month."

The waiter returned and they ordered dinner. When he left, Gerry rested his forearms on the table and said, "I asked you to have dinner with me to get an update on the Valentine ball."

She frowned. "You're up to date. We had a meeting yesterday."

"That was our weekly general office meeting." He leaned forward. "You always tell us about your work in broad strokes. I'd like to get some specifics. I'd like to get a feel for how much work planning an event really is. You tell me flowers are ordered. But I want to know how much work actually goes into ordering flowers, choosing menus, finding a band, all that stuff."

She sat back on her chair. He did not sound like

a man who was retiring. He sounded more like a guy who wanted to replace her.

Uncomfortable, she said, "Everything's sort of intertwined." She paused, trying to think through her answer but her brain was stuck on figuring out why he wanted to replace her.

Unable to come up with a stall, she gave up and decided to tell him what he wanted to know.

"Here's a quick rundown. The staff comes up with a theme for the ball."

"Isn't every Valentine's Day theme love?"

"Yes and no." She fiddled with her napkin. "Remember the one year that everything was silver and white with only red accents?"

He nodded.

"The theme that year was a Winter Wonderland." An idea Ivy had liked so much she decided to use it as the theme of her wedding, except with aqua and blue accents, not red. "The theme determines colors, which determines decorations, which also determines flower choices."

Her phone pinged. She glanced down at it.

Things are getting serious at your table.

He didn't know the half of it.

"After that, the decisions sort of cascade. Once we know the theme, we can determine the menu, choose a band, design decorations and even compile a list of gift bag contents."

He thought for a second. "That makes sense."

Not sure what to say or do, she nodded.

He took a breath. "You came in and took over that position and literally created your own job description."

"You make that sound like a bad thing."

"No. It was a very good thing. But sometimes, like this morning, I realize that most of the time I have no idea what you're doing."

Insulted and confused, she sat up in her chair. "I'm not slacking off if that's what you're insinuating."

He gasped. "Just the opposite. You operate like your own little country." He laughed. "And while that gets great results, if you were hit by a bus or decided to get another job, we'd be lost."

She relaxed, though it did creep her out to think of herself as getting hit by a bus. "I'm not going to leave."

"You say that now, but your events are legendary in the city. I'm surprised someone hasn't approached you with a job offer."

"People have." She shrugged. "I like what I do and want to continue doing it."

Gerry visibly relaxed.

She relaxed.

Her phone pinged.

Everything okay?

The waiter arrived with their food and in the shuffle of plates and bread being set on the table, and water and wine glasses being refilled, she grabbed her phone.

Everything's fine. But this is also a business dinner. I need to focus.

What fun is that?

She looked up from her phone as he glanced over at her, his blue eyes shining. She liked snarky, flirty Jack.

But there was no future for them.

I'm not looking for fun.

Even as she typed those words, she realized how pathetic that sounded.

No wonder he was out of her league. Aside from him, the only thing she ever thought about was work.

CHAPTER SEVEN

SATURDAY NIGHT, JACK unsnapped the cufflinks from his white shirt, then tossed them into the box on the dresser in his massive closet.

Right now, he'd expected to be in Bethany Minor's apartment for after-date drinks that probably would have led to more. But he'd been the worst dinner companion in recorded history. Distracted. Thinking about the texts he'd shared with Autumn at the Italian restaurant. Wondering if she had a date—

It was nuts. And wrong. They'd had their time together. Fate had ruined it…and he'd hurt her. He would not get involved with her again. Period. End of story. Not just because they'd had their one-night stand. But also because he was poison. Not the guy who had long-term relationships. And he refused to hurt her again.

He fell asleep thinking about her and woke Sunday morning restless and bored. After making himself toast and coffee, he pulled out his laptop and started working, but even work couldn't hold his attention.

He thanked God when his phone rang. "Hey, Sebastian! What's up?"

"Ivy's hosting an impromptu brunch. You're invited."

His pulse scrambled. If Ivy was hosting, her best friend would be there.

He told himself not to get excited, then argued that he wasn't going to say or do anything wrong. He simply liked seeing Autumn. He would not make this a big deal.

"Okay. What time?"

"This is impromptu. Put on pants and get here now."

He laughed. "Got it."

He dressed quickly but slowed himself down when he got to the sidewalk in front of his building. He didn't want to look overeager… He was *not* overeager. He just liked her. Liked talking to her. Liked teasing her.

He walked the few blocks to Ivy's townhouse, rang the bell, did a little back and forth with Frances and joined everyone in the big dining room where a buffet was set up along the back wall.

He glanced at the table where a lot of people already sat eating the informal, impromptu bunch—

No Autumn.

Ivy walked over and kissed his cheek. "If you want waffles or an omelet, we can call Louis back to the omelet station. But there's scrambled eggs, sausages, cheese blintzes, toast, bagels in the warmers."

"That sounds great," he said, though his heart sank.

He told himself that was wrong, but it wouldn't lift. He ate some eggs, a blintz and a few sausages, talking and laughing with Ivy's guests and leaving as soon as it was decently polite to do so.

He walked out into the falling snow and looked up. He'd said he'd never be able to see a snowfall again without thinking about her. But he was wrong. He didn't need snow. He simply never stopped thinking about her.

Autumn arrived at her parents' home in time to help her mom put the finishing touches on lunch.

"Where are Aaron and Pete?" she asked as she tied a bib apron over her jeans and white sweater. She didn't care if she got gravy on her jeans—they were washable—but her mother was a stickler about things like aprons, placemats and spoon rests.

"Aaron's mother-in-law is in from Florida and Pete wanted to watch the game in the privacy of his own home."

Autumn held back a laugh. Her dad had a tendency to get vocal and loud when watching the Giants. Pete, a kind, gentle soul, didn't like it.

"So, it's just us?" Autumn picked up the bowl of mashed potatoes and took them to the dining room table, her mom on her heels, carrying the platter of fried chicken.

"Yes. But in a way that's good."

She peered at her mom. "It is?"

"Yes! You rarely talk at our dinners. Your brothers' lives are so interesting that they drown you out." She set down the chicken and looked at her beautifully set table with pride. "It'll be nice to hear about you."

As her mother walked away, Autumn winced. She liked that her brothers monopolized the lunch conversation. That meant she didn't have to lie or embellish what her parents considered her very dull life.

Especially on a day when she was beginning to agree with them.

With everything ready, her mom called her dad and he appeared at the curved archway between the living room and dining room.

"Well, Autumn. Looks like you have us all to yourself today."

"Yes. How's it going, Pop?"

"Same old. Same old. Looking to retire in five years."

"Earlier than most of the guys he works with."

Her mom beamed. "He won't be able to get his pension until he's fifty-nine or government money until he's sixty-two, but we've got savings."

"I know," Autumn agreed, taking her seat in the middle of the left side of the table. With her mom on the right and her dad on the left, she felt like she was in an interrogation room.

Telling herself to shift that focus, she faced her dad. "I've always been proud of your ability to save money."

"Thank your brothers," her dad said, lifting the platter of fried chicken. "They found the investments."

"They're so smart," her mom put in, her face glowing with pride.

In that second, she had the odd urge to brag about how she was so independent at her job that her boss worried she would get hit by a bus, and she couldn't squelch it.

"I had an interesting conversation with my boss the other day."

Her mom brightened. "You did?"

"Yes, he took me to dinner…"

Her dad harrumphed. "I'm not sure I like where this is going."

"Lots of bosses and employees go to dinner. In fact, one of my friends was at the restaurant with two of his vice presidents and their spouses. That was also a business dinner. Happens all the time."

Reminding herself of Jack might not have been the right thing to do. Even though she'd had to shut him down, she'd loved that he'd texted with her. Flirted with her, really—

She'd promised herself she wouldn't make too much of that.

But now that she'd reminded herself of it, her brain smiled.

Her mother said, "Tell us about the dinner. Are you getting a raise?"

Glad to be brought back to the present, she said, "No. My boss told me that I do so much that most of the time he doesn't even know what I'm doing."

Her dad waved his fork. "That happens all the time with secretaries."

Her nerves tweaked. The way he thought she was a secretary made her crazy. "I'm not a secretary. I'm in charge of all the event planning. I supervise the mentors."

The table fell silent. Autumn picked up her fork and snared a bite of her chicken, refusing to get angry. Her parents were old school. If a woman worked in an office, she was a secretary or assistant. They couldn't get beyond that and Autumn couldn't change fifty years of conditioning.

"It doesn't matter, dear," her mom said. "One of these days you'll find a nice young man and settle down."

She took a breath. They'd been over this a thousand times. "Mom, it isn't that I don't want to get married." It simply wasn't in her life plan. "Right now, I'm focused on my career. I know you guys don't understand my job but it's pretty important and what I do makes a difference."

"You know who makes a difference?" her dad asked, stabbing his fork at her. "Your brothers. That's how I got savings enough to retire. That's why Aaron has that big house in Connecticut. That's making a difference."

"And making money," her mom agreed.

Autumn nodded. They might not understand her job, but she did and that was what mattered.

"So, any nice young men in your life?"

She said, "No." But Jack was. Sort of. They had a dance lesson tomorrow and maybe another one before they'd spend Friday night at the rehearsal dinner and Saturday at the wedding.

She didn't want to be excited over that. But, surely, she could admit to herself that she liked him as a friend.

That didn't sound too bad.

And thinking about him, about spending time with him, about how silly he'd been with the texting, was more fun than having her parents diss her job and ask about boyfriends she didn't have.

For goodness sake, she wasn't even looking for a boyfriend. Which might be why Jack was so appealing. He wasn't looking at her as a girlfriend. They'd had their shot and he'd ended it.

There'd never be anything serious between them.

But did that mean they couldn't have some fun?

Her dad went on chattering about her successful brothers as her mom chimed in with other wonderful accomplishments of her two male siblings and she thought about Jack.

And everybody at the table was happy.

When Jack arrived at the dance studio on Monday night, Autumn was seated on the bench changing into her ballet slippers. The door closed behind him and she glanced over. Their gazes caught and held. A million feelings rippled through him, mostly happiness at seeing her. But that was wrong.

He broke their connection and slipped out of his overcoat, then his jacket and tie. As he rolled his shirt sleeves to his elbows, Greg came out of the back room.

"Okay, favorite couple. Are we ready to tackle that Charleston step?"

Jack winced. "Actually, I looked it up on YouTube. I should ace it now."

Greg laughed. "Better to look it up than to worry about being embarrassed."

"Exactly."

"All right then. Let's take it from the top."

Without a word, Autumn lined up at the edge of the dance floor and Jack joined her. Greg started the music.

Jack took Autumn's hand and twirled her out to the center. They looked left then right, did five perfect Charleston steps, then he pulled her into his arms for the waltz.

As Greg had instructed them, they looked into each other's eyes. He told himself they had only done it because Greg had told them they had to, but there was something more in Autumn's eyes tonight. Something curious and inviting.

He waltzed her around the circle of the dance floor, flowing with her as if they were floating, as if they were made to be dance partners. Something deep and profound seemed to connect them. For twenty seconds, there was no one else in the room.

They stopped, but she didn't try to slide out of his arms, and he didn't try to pull away. They simply stared at each other.

Greg clapped. "That was magnificent! My God, Jack, you were born to waltz and Autumn you were born to twirl."

She pulled away, laughing at Greg. "Born to twirl? Really? You sound like my mom and dad."

"In the world of dance being born to twirl is

not an insult. It's me telling you that you probably don't need another lesson."

She walked over and hugged him. "I know. I'm sorry. I had lunch with my parents yesterday and they always make me overthink everything anyone says."

He batted a hand. "I have parents too. I know the drill."

She laughed again as Jack sauntered over to them. "So, should we take it from the top?"

"Only if you want to," Greg said happily. "You two are gorgeous together."

Autumn's face reddened. "I wouldn't go that far."

"I would. But if you want to continue practicing, the floor is yours for fifteen more minutes. If not, I will be rooting for you at the wedding."

"You're going to the wedding?"

"Ivy's a family friend. She and my wife are on some board together."

Autumn glanced at Jack and she smiled an I-told-you-so smile. They'd discussed the possibility that Ivy had looked for ways to force them together. Her connection to Greg just about sealed it.

"I don't think we need to run through it again," he said, peeking at Autumn. "Unless you do."

"No. I'm fine."

"Then maybe we could have coffee. There's

a little place down the street." When she didn't reply, he added, "There are a few things I need to tell you."

The curiosity returned to her eyes, but this time there was no invitation. Only caution. Still, she said, "Okay," and walked to the bench to change her shoes while he put on his suit jacket and overcoat.

This time the tension that skimmed his nerve endings wasn't excitement. It was a day-of-reckoning feeling. He'd hurt her. He owed her an explanation, even though he knew full well telling her the truth about their night together would end their attraction.

But that was for the best.

CHAPTER EIGHT

THE COFFEE SHOP Jack had mentioned was only two buildings down from the dance studio. When they reached it, he pushed open the door and let her enter before him.

Not sure what to expect from this conversation, Autumn began to slip out of her jacket.

Edging toward the counter of the crowded business, he said, "What can I get you?"

The gesture was simple and maybe even okay given that the place was filled with people on phones and laptops and lines for coffee were long. Still, he'd been weird at the dance studio and she had no idea what he was about to tell her. Best to keep their roles clear.

"I'll get my own."

"No. The place is too full. You get a seat. I'll get the coffee. What do you want?"

She glanced around. Technically, there was only one table with two open seats. She'd let him win this one. "Caramel macchiato."

She wove her way between tables and people

to the two high stools at the open table and sat, pulling out her phone as he ordered. No missed calls. No voice mails. Nothing to take her focus away from the fact that he'd said he had a *few things* to tell her.

Of course, she hoped he wanted to explain why he'd left and never called all those years ago. But that was wishful thinking. Lots of time might have passed, but she wanted to know. At the same time, that lots of time had been *five years.* He could think it irrelevant.

Still, if she eliminated that possibility completely, she had no idea what he wanted to talk about.

She groaned at the way her thoughts had become uncontrollable since he'd reentered her life, before she looked down at her phone and began reading the news.

A few minutes later, he appeared at the table.

He set her drink in front of her. "Caramel macchiato."

"Wow. The big one. Somebody's not sleeping tonight."

He winced. "Sorry."

She waved a hand. "Sleep is overrated." She frowned. "Where's yours?"

"Actually, I sort of just wanted to explain something and then leave."

Well, that didn't sound good.

Particularly when his words coupled with the somber expression on his face.

"I wasn't going to explain why I left you that night." He shook his head. "Five years had passed. It seemed... I don't know...irrelevant?"

She'd thought that. But her curiosity spiked, and her nerve endings sat at full attention. "Maybe five years means it won't annoy me as much as it would have if you'd told me right away."

He sniffed a laugh.

Her overly active brain began remembering the conclusions she'd drawn in the weeks after he never called. He'd met someone else. An old love had returned, and he'd realized he still loved her. An old love had returned and told him she was pregnant. An old love had returned holding his baby in her arms—

"I got up in the middle of the night and for whatever reason, I turned on my phone."

So, an old girlfriend had *called* while they'd had their phones off.

"It was the hospital."

That surprised her so much her brain stopped drawing conclusions.

"My mom had been admitted and they needed me to come down immediately."

And, at her apartment, he'd been almost an hour away in Queens.

"What had happened?"

He took a breath and, seeming exhausted, he slid onto the chair across from her. "She'd had a heart attack. She'd already died by the time I called. I don't know if they weren't allowed to tell me that over the phone, or if something had gotten screwed up. But I raced to the hospital."

She could only stare at him. Remorse filled her. Along with nearly overwhelming compassion for him. "Oh, my God, I'm so sorry."

"I was stunned. She was in her fifties. Healthy. No. She was robust. She was one of those people who had tons of energy. She'd started Step Inside. It was her baby. Her vision. I was the chef for the original restaurant, then I eased into research and development, but the day after her funeral, I had ten restaurants to run."

She leaned back on her chair. "That's a lot."

"It was. She had a good assistant and a knowledgeable vice president who operated as chief financial officer. They literally taught me the ropes of the business."

She remembered him saying something about a five-year plan at Ivy and Sebastian's house, and realized that for the past five years he'd been building his mother's dream.

"You sort of dropped off my radar."

She had no idea what to say. He'd been a chef forced to become a businessman and he'd done a great job if the little she knew about Step Inside was anything to go by. But he'd also lost his mom—

And he had no brothers and sisters. He'd told her he was an only child.

"I'm so sorry."

He slid off the stool. "That's it. That's what I wanted to tell you. It's clear that we like each other but I knew we'd never really ever be able to even be friends if I didn't tell you."

Not knowing what to say, she took a breath before she settled on, "I'm glad you did."

He sort of smiled, nodded and headed for the door.

She watched him walk out into the few flurries of snow that swirled in a light breeze. He flipped up his collar and headed down the street to his car.

She stared straight ahead, her caramel macchiato forgotten.

Technically, he was all alone in the world.

Autumn was so gobsmacked by Jack's revelation that she wondered about him all week. Even standing outside the restaurant for the rehearsal dinner, she thought about him while waiting for her parents. It was a tradition in Ivy's family that the parents of the entire bridal party also be invited to the wedding and rehearsal dinner. Her dad had driven into the city and her latest text from her mom said they were walking up the street.

She glanced left and right, then winced. She didn't want to run into Jack out on the street, where they'd be alone, and conversation would be awkward. She wanted the protection of other wedding participants, so they didn't have that awkward moment where he realized she knew his secrets. She knew his past. She knew his pain.

She wasn't uncomfortable with it. But from the way he'd left the coffee shop, she knew he was.

Her parents came bounding up the street. Her mom's cheeks were red from the cold. Dressed in his best overcoat and only suit, her dad looked like he'd rather be shot than enter the restaurant.

She straightened the collar of his overcoat. "Ivy's parents might be wealthy, but they are very nice."

Her dad rolled his eyes.

"Sebastian grew up middle class."

"Thought his dad was a lawyer."

"He is, but not all lawyers are wealthy." Though Sebastian's company had taken his dad's mediocre law firm and made it great when it became the firm's biggest client.

She decided to change tactics. "This is a totally mixed crowd of people. You're going to love them."

Her mom nodded happily. Her dad sighed.

They walked into the restaurant where the maî-tre d' motioned for someone to get their coats, then led them to the private room for the rehearsal dinner.

Ivy's and Sebastian's parents stood at the door greeting guests. Ivy's mom, Lydia, with the same short black hair and green eyes as Ivy, immedi-ately reached out and took Autumn's hands be-fore kissing both of her cheeks. "It's so lovely to see you again, darling."

"Thanks, Lydia."

Ivy's dad stepped forward, hugging Autumn. "And who are these two?" he asked referring to Autumn's parents.

"Lydia, Robert, these are my parents. Mary and Jim."

Robert immediately shook Autumn's dad's hand. He motioned to Sebastian's parents, who were chatting with another couple, but turned around when they realized more people had come to the door. "These are Sebastian's parents. Mike and Emily."

Mike and Emily shook everyone's hand. "Such a pleasure to meet you. We've heard a great deal about your daughter from Sebastian."

Another couple entered behind them and Au-tumn said, "I'm sure we'll have a minute to chat later." Then she led her parents away from the door and into the small group of round tables with elegant white linen tablecloths and centerpieces made with bright red Christmas ornaments arranged in bouquets of white flowers. Some couples had already seated themselves. Others stood between the tables talking.

She immediately homed in on her parents' place cards. "It looks like you're sitting here."

Her mother frowned. "Where are you sitting?"

"I'm in the bridal party. I'll probably be at the main table," she said, pointing to a table at the head of the room.

"We'll be alone?"

"You're sitting with six other people."

"Jim?"

A tall, barrel-chested man approached her dad. He extended his hand to shake Jim's. "What the heck are you doing here?"

To Autumn's surprise, her dad laughed. "My daughter's in the wedding." Jim turned and introduced Autumn and her mom to Paul Fabian. "We used to work together."

Mary said, "Really?"

Jim snorted. "Yeah, then he got the bright idea to buy a business."

"Sebastian's dad handled the deal and we've been friends ever since. My daughter's a flower girl." He glanced around. "Where are you sitting?"

Her dad pointed. "Here."

"So are we. I'll go get my wife."

He was back in the blink of an eye, but Autumn barely noticed. Jack entered, kissed Ivy's mom's cheek, shook hands with her dad and moved on to Sebastian's parents.

He looked amazing in a dark suit with a white shirt and a blue tie. The night she'd met him, she'd felt like she'd been struck by lightning. Tonight, a lot of those same feelings came tumbling back, but so did respect and an odd kind of empathy. She knew what it was like to fight her way through life. Now, she knew he did too.

The small room filled quickly, and Sebastian's dad announced that everyone should find their seats. She eased to the bridal table and wasn't surprised that she and Jack were seated next to each other.

"Hey."

He pulled his seat closer to the table. "Hey."

He seemed uncomfortable so she said the first thing that popped into her head. "How was your week?"

He glanced at her as if to remind her they'd spent bits and pieces of that week together, including the hour-long rehearsal only a few minutes before, where they'd learned their part for the wedding ceremony.

Eventually he said, "Exhausting."

She ignored the one-word answer that might

have been a sign that he didn't want to talk. Their
entire relationship had been built on drama. First,
the lightning strike when they met. Going home
together. Him getting a call that his mom was
in the hospital, only to discover she was already
gone. Her waking up alone. Then not seeing each
other again for five years.

Maybe it was time to drop the drama and behave like normal people. "Mine was exhausting
too." She faced him fully. "I spent most of it wondering about that dinner I had with my boss."

Obviously glad she wasn't going to talk about
what he'd told her at the coffee shop, he perked
up. "Oh, yeah. Why?"

"He told me he didn't exactly know my job."
She paused, took a breath. "I should probably start
at the beginning. Gerry is retirement age. When
he told me we needed a private conversation, I
thought he was going to tell me he was retiring
and I was in line for his position."

Jack's brain clicked with a new memory. He'd remembered she'd talked about her job but couldn't
remember everything she'd said. Now, he recalled
her mentioning to him that someday she wanted
to run the charity where she worked. She wanted
to be CEO. She wanted to prove herself.

He waited for the recollection from that night to
sour his stomach or make him feel guilty. Instead,

it felt like a breath of fresh air—or like a clearing of the uncomfortable air that always hung between them. Maybe what they needed was a little more normal conversation about inconsequential things to whisk away the power that night seemed to hold over them.

He shifted on his chair to face her. "I sort of remember that. But I take it that wasn't why he'd wanted an out of the office meeting."

"No. I got the impression he felt odd about not knowing exactly what I do."

"What do you do?"

"Lots. My job overlaps. I plan and execute all events, but I also monitor the mentors and the cases they handle. That way, I know exactly what we're doing and can also be the PR person."

"Wow. You raise the money, talk to the press and handle clients?"

She inclined her head. "Yes."

"Do you have any accounting experience?"

A white-coated waiter stopped to fill his glass with champagne before he filled Autumn's. As if wanting privacy, she waited until he had moved on to the next couple in the bridal party before she said, "I took classes at university but never did the job."

He considered that. "Your boss might have been feeling you out to see if you are a candidate to replace him. You know the business. You

have a basic understanding of the accounting."
He shrugged. "I wouldn't worry too much about
the meeting."

"Thanks."

He barely had time to say, "You're welcome,"
before the toasts began.

Ivy's toast to her future husband was funny.
Sebastian's toast to Ivy was sentimental and romantic.

After the meal, the rehearsal dinner went on in
an almost ordinary fashion, with people leaving
their tables and mingling. He talked with Sebastian's best man Gio then Sebastian's dad. Then
found himself in a group of laughing people. Autumn stood in the circle, enjoying the crowd, and
the mixed feelings he had about her when they
first sat down together dissolved even more. She
loved to laugh, and he loved hearing her laugh.

She didn't seem crushed or embarrassed or
even guilty at having heard the story of his mom.
But he supposed she shouldn't. They hadn't really
known each other that night. And though she'd
been sad about his mom's passing and truly had
seemed concerned about him, the way she'd spoken so normally to him had soothed wounds he
didn't even remember he had.

Suddenly he could put a name to the feeling
he had around her.

Normalcy.

She made him feel normal.

He'd spent his entire life being slightly off center. After his dad had abandoned him and his mom, there were only the two of them and they'd formed a team. At little league and soccer, he hadn't been an outcast. There were lots of single parent kids. But he'd always been *that* kid whose father had left and started another family, as if Jack and his mom were somehow substandard. Then he'd become a chef and quickly rose to be everybody's boss at the business his mom owned. Then she'd died and *he'd* owned the business. Hundreds of people depended on him for a living. Plus, he'd had a dream to fulfill. His mom's.

He'd never had a minute to breathe and just be himself.

She let him be himself.

People began to leave. Sebastian and Ivy stood at the door, excited for the big day and telling everyone they would see them at the wedding.

As the crowd thinned, Jack also walked to the door, telling Ivy and Sebastian he would be at the townhouse first thing in the morning, and ambling over to the coatroom.

An older man and woman were sliding into jackets beside Autumn who already wore her black wool coat.

As he stepped inside, Autumn said, "Mom, Dad, this is Jack. He's my partner in the wedding."

He shook Autumn's dad's hand and said, "It's nice to meet you."

Her mom said, "So you're Autumn's partner?"

"Yes. For the wedding. She knows Ivy. I know Sebastian."

Her mom beamed. "It's going to be so beautiful."

"Ivy has impeccable taste," he agreed.

Autumn gathered her parents and headed for the door. "Time to go. You still have a long drive ahead of you."

Jack said, "You drove?"

Autumn's dad puffed out his chest. "I've been driving into this city for forty years. No reason not to."

Impressed, Jack nodded. Autumn said, "We'll see you, Jack." Then got her parents out the door.

He grabbed his overcoat, slid into it and walked out of the restaurant to the sidewalk, where Autumn stood alone.

He frowned. "Where are your parents?"

"Walking to their car."

He peered down the street. "Where'd they park?"

She laughed. "I don't know."

"Are they coming back to pick you up?"

"No. They live in Hunter. I live in Queens."

He glanced down the street again. "Oh."

"Don't ask me if I need a ride. I have a car coming."

He almost chuckled. She was so predictable in her need to be her own person. But he supposed he understood that now that she'd reminded him about her desire to rise to the top of her organization. She was capable and didn't want anyone to minimize that. "Okay."

"And you can go. I don't need a babysitter."

His lips lifted. She was so adamant in her independence, it never occurred to her that he wanted to stay to get some time with her. "What about someone to keep you company?"

She frowned as if that confused her.

"Come on. It could be fifteen or twenty minutes before your ride gets here. It's better to have company. I can give you my opinion on what your boss was thinking at dinner the other night."

"You already did."

"Okay. We can talk about the wedding."

"You want to talk about flower girl dresses and silver decorations that sparkle?"

He grimaced. "Probably not."

"How about the decision that the bridesmaids should wear champagne-colored dresses?"

He laughed. "Lord, no."

"I didn't think so."

"I am curious about what you've been doing the past five years."

She stiffened defensively. "Why? Because I'm still in the same job?"

"No. Because five years is a long time, and you aren't the same, but you aren't really different either."

She shrugged. "It would be odd if I hadn't changed at least a bit in five years."

"Yeah. I guess."

He looked up the street and down again, trying to think of something to say. What came to him surprised him, but he knew he had to say it. "When we're together like this, you know, kind of by ourselves, I realize that I missed you over the past five years. Just never really knew it."

"You couldn't miss me. You didn't know me. And you were mourning your mom as you worked your butt off. There was no room for me."

"That's just it. I always had this little tweak way deep down inside. I think that was the memory of you trying to surface but not being able to because of all the other things bogging me down."

She laughed but her heart almost exploded from the romance of it. The night they'd met he'd swept her off her feet with simple sincerity. He had a way of looking at things, phrasing things, that was so honest she knew he truly believed what he said.

Not accustomed to anyone having that kind of feelings for her, she brushed it off. "That's silly."

He took a step closer. "Really?"

Her breath stuttered. Memories of their first kiss tumbled into her brain. How much she'd liked him. How eager she'd been for him to kiss her. The same feelings coursed through her now. Stealing her breath. Prickling along her nerve endings.

"I'd never met anybody like you before. Never experienced the love-at-first-sight feeling." He edged closer. "I was so smitten, and you were so perfect." He slid his hands to her shoulders. "How could you not have known only a real disaster would have blotted you out of my mind?"

He bent his head and brushed his lips across hers. Just like the first time he'd kissed her, she totally melted. He eased his mouth along hers a few times, raising goose bumps and igniting something hot and sweet deep inside her. Memories of their past drifted into nothing, as the present drove away everything but the feeling of him against her and the way their mouths fit so perfectly.

Dangerous longing woke in her soul. She'd felt this before and he'd left her. But right now, he was very solid under the hands she had gripping his biceps, as his tempting mouth teased her into believing every wonderful word he said.

The honk of a horn broke them apart. She

glanced up to see the light blue sedan from her ride share request.

She pulled away but had to swallow before she could say, "That's my ride."

"You sure you don't want me to take you home?"

And have another goodnight kiss? One that might lead her to invite him inside? For a night of wonderful sex, deep, personal conversations and a dollop of silliness?

Her heart stumbled. Fear of rejection battled with yearning.

The car honked again.

She'd made this decision lightly once. She would not make it lightly again.

"I want to be rested for the wedding."

He laughed, then ran his hand along her hair. "If past experience is anything to go by we'd be walking zombies tomorrow if we went home together."

She held his gaze almost wishing they could have another night. That she could be strong enough to face the inevitable rejection.

But she knew she couldn't.

She headed to the ride share. "See you tomorrow."

His smiled, but his eyes filled with regret. "See you tomorrow."

CHAPTER NINE

SEBASTIAN AND IVY'S wedding was the most beautiful Autumn had ever seen. Men always looked resplendent in tuxes. But with four gentlemen as handsome as Sebastian, his brother-in-law, the best man Gio and, of course, Jack, she would bet the pulse of every woman in the room had scrambled.

Ivy's mom had forgone the typical pink for the bride's mother and had chosen a rich burgundy dress in a simple A-line style that cruised her tall, slim figure. Sebastian's mom wore an icy sapphire dress that suited her skin tone and white hair to perfection.

Add all those black tuxes and the champagne-colored dresses of the bridesmaids to the Winter Wonderland theme of the reception venue and Autumn truly felt she was in an enchanted forest. Well placed lights dramatized the small evergreens that had been sprinkled with silver glitter and scattered throughout the room. Round tables covered in linen cloths as white as snow held centerpieces of frosted evergreen adorned with blue and aqua Christmas ornaments. A huge white wedding cake sparkled in the center of the room. Accent lights of blue and aqua took turns illuminating the glittering confection, making it look like magic.

But the real beauty was Ivy. Wearing a simple white velvet gown and white floral fascinator with netting that angled down one side of her forehead, she looked like a princess or the heroine from a fairytale. Slim, tall, regal. Her face glowed when she looked at Sebastian.

Jack slid his hand along the small of Autumn's back. "How long *is* this reception line?"

Though the feeling of his palm on her bare back sent shivers through her, she casually replied. "I don't know. Every time I turned around the guest list changed. I have no idea how many people are here."

He chuckled and temptation to look at him overwhelmed her. She glanced at him and let her breath stall at how sexy he looked in a tux. But just like the night of the gala—when he had been the most gorgeous man in attendance—she didn't feel less than. That night she'd worn one of Ivy's gowns and knew she looked as good as she felt. Tonight, she wore a backless dress. The high collar in the front was slenderizing. The dip of the back that slid the whole way down, stopping only three or four inches above her bottom, was sophisticatedly sexy.

If there was ever a night she truly felt his equal it was tonight.

For a few minutes there was chaos as the reception line continued and guests found their seats. Autumn shifted the beautiful bouquet the florist, Hailey, had made from her right hand to her left and back again, accepting hugs and greeting guests as they walked from the bride and groom to the bridal party.

When the line slimmed to thirty or so people, she and Jack skirted the edge of the room to go to the bridal table on a platform on the far end. Working to keep the confusion to a minimum, they sat as soon as they reached their chairs. Sebastian's sister and brother-in-law did too. And soon Gio and the maid of honor followed.

Ivy and Sebastian walked into the noisy room, a spotlight finding them for guests and following them. The room fell silent. They walked up an aisle created in the center of the round tables that led to the bridal table, while a version of "Silvery Moon" played. It was both a nod to Ivy's dad who loved old music and the theme of the room. Autumn marveled at the beautiful job done by wedding planner Alexandra.

The bride and groom seated themselves at the bridal table, laughing, holding hands. Gio immediately took his glass of champagne and de-livered his toast.

But Autumn's gaze kept sliding to Jack, and his arm kept sliding to the back of her chair. They were like a magnet and metal. If they were close, they wanted to touch. She'd fought it the night before, through the ceremony and the wedding photos. She could be strong now too.

Gio finished his toast and to everyone's surprise Sebastian's sister rose to give a toast to her brother. Her comments were light and silly, making Sebastian laugh and his parents sit like two proud peacocks.

Champagne flowed like water. The whole room shimmered as if it had been touched by an angel.

Dinner was served, then Ivy and Sebastian cut the big white cake in the center of the room and it was distributed to the guests along with a small box containing the cakes made as a favor for each guest.

The room buzzed with appreciation and happiness. Ivy and Sebastian left the bridal table and mingled for a minute as the band returned. Then the MC announced their first dance and Ivy and Sebastian glided onto the floor.

Autumn sighed. "They look made for each other."

Jack said, "They are."

"When her dad retires, her life's not going to be easy."

"Sure, it will," he said, refilling her champagne glass from a magnum left by one of the waiters at Jack's request. "Sebastian's already working on software that will do most of her work."

She laughed and drank a little more of the delicious champagne before she turned to him. "We can't drink too much of this. We have a dance to do. In fact, I promised we'd practice before our performance."

"No need. Thanks to YouTube. Plus, there's no time for practice."

"True. We should probably head to the dance floor now to be ready once Ivy and Sebastian's dance is over."

Jack rose and pulled out her chair. "Let's go."

They eased off the raised platform of the bridal table and walked along the edge of the room until they were parallel with the dance floor.

The song shifted to the bridal party dance and Jack and Autumn hurried to get to the rim of the dance floor.

"And now here's the bridal party." The MC motioned for them to come forward. "First, bridesmaid Autumn Jones and groomsman Jack Adams."

Jack expertly twirled her out onto the floor. Then they faced each other, looked left and looked right. She twirled to stand beside him. They did five perfect Charleston steps and then he slid his hand across her bare back again, putting them in the waltz position to dance them over to Ivy and Sebastian.

Remembering Greg's training, she linked her gaze to Jack's and everything inside her stilled. Every time she touched him, every time she looked into his eyes, she felt a connection so strong she wondered if they hadn't been lovers in another life.

The music flowed and Jack smoothly led them around the floor, his hand resting on the bare flesh of her back. She tried to focus her attention away from the way her nerve endings sparked, sending desire through her. But it was no use. Their chemistry was off the charts.

And maybe it was foolish to ignore that?

With their gazes locked, and whirling around the large dance floor as if they were made to be partners, it definitely seemed foolish to ignore it. What would it be like to roll the dice and see where this would go?

They finally reached Ivy and Sebastian. Their steps slowed, then stopped as they settled in beside the happy bride and groom, and Sebastian's sister and brother-in-law took the floor. After their few fun dance steps, they waltzed over to

Jack and Autumn, stopping so close, they nudged Autumn up against Jack's side.

As if it were the most natural thing in the world, he slid his arm across her shoulders, making room for Sebastian's sister and brother-in-law.

Gio and his partner took the floor, did their steps and waltzed over. The dance ended. The MC introduced them again and they took a bow, before the band began playing a song designed to get people out of their seats and onto the dance floor.

It filled in seconds. Ivy and Sebastian headed into the crowd to mingle. Sebastian's sister and brother-in-law danced their way back to the floor. Gio disappeared.

Jack slid his arm from around her shoulders, as someone walked up to him. Clearly a business acquaintance, he motioned for Jack to move to a quieter area and then he was gone.

It seemed odd at first that he'd left her side. Being partners meant they'd been together all day. But this was the party portion of the program. They were no longer obligated to be together.

Her heart tweaked with disappointment, but she took a breath and found her parents who were still seated at their table. She asked her dad if he wanted a drink and plucked two glasses of champagne off the tray of a passing waiter.

"So fancy," her mom said reverently.

Her dad mumbled, "I'd rather have a beer."

"Let me take you over to the bar. I'm guessing Ivy has everything any guest could want."

He rose from the table.

"Wanna come, Ma?"

"No. I think I'll just sit here, sip my champagne and enjoy how beautiful everything is."

Temptation rippled through her. She nearly told her mom that Ivy's wedding might be top of the line, but she planned galas every bit as elegant for Raise Your Voice.

Still, she knew her mom didn't want to hear that. She walked her dad to the bar and after he got his favorite beer, they turned to go back to his seat. But Ivy stopped her.

She caught her hand and pulled her toward the dance floor. "I love this song. Come on. Dance with me."

Her dad motioned for her to go. "If I can find my way in this enormous city, I can find my way back to the table."

"You're sure?"

"Your mom and I aren't dorks."

Ivy laughed. "Your dad has a point."

"Okay. I'll be back after this song, Dad."

"No. You go have fun."

For once his words didn't sound condescending. Though she watched him as he returned to his table, he easily found his way.

She threw herself into the dance with Ivy and one dance turned into three before Sebastian joined them. Feeling like a third wheel, she eased away and bumped into Gerry and his wife.

"Such a beautiful wedding!" Gerry's wife gushed. "And you look perfect! Wonderful!"

She blushed. "Thanks. Ivy has good taste."

"And you have good bones," Gerry's wife said. "I always knew that outside of that office you went from a duckling into a swan."

"Matilda!"

"What? Lots of women dress down for their job. It's a matter of being respected for the work they do. Not how they look." She reached out and pinched Autumn's cheek. "But outside the office? She's a glamour girl."

Autumn snorted. "Not a glamour girl."

"Ha!" Matilda said. "You cannot say that with a straight face tonight. I'm doing the same thing when Gerry and I move to Florida. I might have been dowdy here, but once we get our condo I'm going to dress up. We'll be the youngest of the old people down there and I will be fabulous."

Gerry groaned and shook his head.

Matilda frowned. "What? I'm talking about when you retire."

Though she laughed at Matilda's enthusiasm, the mention of Gerry's retirement caused Autumn's eyebrows to rise.

Gerry groaned again. "This is neither the time nor the place."

Matilda shrugged. "Whatever."

Gerry leaned into Autumn and said, "She's had a little champagne."

"It *is* good champagne."

"Marvelous champagne," Matilda said.

Gerry motioned to the door. "I think we might be leaving early."

Autumn said, "Have a safe trip home," watching them as they made their way through the crowd out of the ballroom to the coatroom. When she added Gerry's surprise dinner at the Italian restaurant to Matilda's happy thoughts about retiring in Florida, her breath stuttered with hope. What if he was in the planning stages for retirement? What if all of her career goals were about to materialize?

She told herself not to get ahead of things.

Still, she could almost see her name on the door to the CEO's office. This time next year, she could be running the charity that meant so much to her.

Her shoulders shifted back. Her chest filled with excitement.

She was doing it. She was accomplishing what she'd set out to do. She was the woman she'd always wanted to be.

She spent more time with her parents, even persuading her mom to dance. Then, drifting through the room, she chatted with other members of the Raise Your Voice staff who had been invited to the wedding, a new confidence rippling through her.

Her gaze found Jack in the crowd a few times. Once or twice their eyes had met. And he'd smiled at her as if they had a secret—

Well, technically they did. She hadn't gotten around to telling Ivy they already knew each other. And from the lack of comment from Sebastian or Ivy she suspected Jack hadn't either.

She returned his smile before she was pulled away by some employees of Raise Your Voice to dance. Far too soon, Ivy and Sebastian did their final dance, then took the microphone to thank everyone for coming and he carried her out of the venue and to a waiting limo. Everyone applauded and the band continued playing, but the night was drawing to a close.

She helped her parents get their coats and waved goodbye to them from the entryway as they waited for the valet to get their car.

She raced back to the big ballroom, hoping to dance the last few songs, and almost ran into Jack. "Hey."

"I thought you might be leaving."

"Nope, just sending the parents off."

"They're nice people."

"They told me you found them and had a chat."

He winced. "Nothing serious."

The band announced the last song of the evening and her heart sunk but Jack said, "Wanna dance?"

New, confident Autumn who'd been lurking under the surface all along said, "Sure. I'd love to."

He pulled her into his arms for the slow song and she melted into him. The connection was stunning. They didn't merely have chemistry. They truly liked each other...and she was a little tired of fighting something she wanted.

"I stayed away from you through the night to give you a chance to mingle."

She leaned back to look at him. "Really?"

"Sure. People from your office were here. So was your board of directors."

She wrinkled her nose. "I steered clear of them."

He chuckled. "I thought you'd take the opportunity to suck up to them."

She laughed joyously. It felt ridiculously wonderful that the universe seemed to be lining up for her. Career plans materializing. The man she wanted gazing at her adoringly.

If there was ever a time to be herself, to take instead of wait, this was it.

To hell with worry that she couldn't handle another rejection. If she looked at this as a one-night stand, a chance to be with a wonderful man again, she wouldn't get hurt.

She wasn't that naive anymore.

She sucked in a breath, marshalled her courage and said, "Want to come back to my apartment?"

He smiled hopefully. "Mine's closer."

Anticipation built then exploded. Her life had never been so perfect. No man had ever been so perfect.

"Sounds good to me."

CHAPTER TEN

JACK SHOT A quick text to Arnie and his limo was outside the wedding venue in a few minutes. He and Autumn slid into the back. He raised the partition between the driver and the passengers, then pulled her to him for a long, lush kiss.

Everything inside him told him this was right. He'd considered making the suggestion himself, but he needed to be sure this was what she wanted. Having her ask—without even a dropped hint from him—proved they were on the same page.

When they arrived at his building, he ushered her through the ornate lobby and into the elevator, where he kissed her again. The doors opened on his penthouse and they kissed their way through the living room and down the hall to the bedroom where they tumbled onto his California king bed.

It amazed him that a dress that essentially had no back, also gave no clue as to how he was supposed to get it off.

She broke their kiss, reached up and undid

three almost invisible buttons that fastened in the back of the high band around her neck. Then she let them go and the front of the dress billowed down, exposing her creamy skin.

His breath caught. Reverence for the moment wrestled with need.

She didn't give him time to think. She slid her hands under his jacket, over his shoulders and slipped it down his arms. He shucked it off, then undid his tie and began to unbutton his shirt.

She slapped his hands away. "That's my fun."

"I let you unbutton your dress…"

"Yeah, because you couldn't find the buttons!"

"They were craftily hidden." He laughed, then kissed her as she worked her way down the buttons of his shirt. When she reached the last one, she yanked the shirt out of his trousers and he rose, reaching for his belt.

"If you want to get fancy, we can do it another time. I've waited too long. Remembered too many wonderful things." He slid out of his pants and sat beside her on the bed. "I want you now."

Longing shuddered through Autumn. She wanted him too. But it was more the things he said that filled her with need. How could she not be comfortable with a man who called their last night together wonderful?

The best of his life.

He pushed her back on the bed, then gave one quick yank that slid her dress off. His lips met the sensitive skin of her neck as his hand fell to her breast and she groaned with pleasure, smoothing her hands down his back, enjoying the solidness of the muscle and flesh.

But everything seemed off somehow and she realized they were too sedate. They'd played like two warring tiger cubs their last night together. And that's what she wanted. She wanted them desperate and assertive. So eager to have fun that politeness was not invited into their game.

With a quick jab against his shoulder, she shifted him enough that he rolled to his back and she straddled him. Before he could react, she brought her mouth to his neck. He groaned, but she bit and teased until a quick move from him reversed their positions again.

She laughed. This was what she wanted. The raw honesty.

He ran his hands over her quickly, hungrily, as he suckled her breast. The crazy need that had cruised her nerve endings burst into fire. Putting her hands on his cheeks, she lifted his face for a kiss that went from hot to scorching so fast she didn't even realize he'd positioned himself to take her.

The unexpectedness of it sent lightning through her. Their scorching kiss ramped up another notch. His pace became frantic. Need swelled to a pleasure pain that exploded into almost unbearable joy. She felt his release immediately after, as ripple after ripple of aftershock stole her breath.

He rolled away and she closed her eyes savoring the sweet feeling of complete satisfaction and the happiness at realizing she had not imagined the intensity and fun of their first night all those years ago.

As if to reinforce that, he angled her to him and kissed her deeply.

"That was nice."

She disagreed. "That was explosive."

Their legs tangled. She smiled. He smiled, then kissed her again. He broke the kiss and nestled her against him. The simplicity of it warmed her, as they all but purred with satisfaction. Her ridiculously high comfort level with him relaxed her to the point that she could have fallen asleep. After the long day that they'd had, sleep seemed like a good idea. Cuddled next to him, with his arm around her protectively and his whole body brushing hers, she felt like she was in heaven.

His hand skimmed her spine. Her hands trickled up his chest. Desire began to hum and build until the next thing she knew they were making love again. Kissing deeply, their bodies gliding against each other sensually. The slower movements suited them as well as the frenetic love-making had. But as the need grew, light touches became caresses. Inquisitive hands became bold. They only needed to roll together to connect again. The arousal so deep and profound it rose to a pitch that couldn't be sustained. It burst like a hot bubble that rained pleasure through her. She gasped for breath and let it take her.

This time when they cuddled, she swore she could feel his happiness. Everything about their first night together came into focus again. Why she'd been so sure they were about to become an item. Why it had been so devastating when he hadn't called.

Her eyes closed. She told herself none of that mattered. She did not want to fall into that pit again where her expectations didn't match what actually happened. Especially since her own life was up in the air right now.

He ran his lips from her neck to her belly button. "We are ridiculously hot together. And fast. That could be construed as a bad thing, but I've never felt anything so intense that I couldn't control it. And I liked letting go."

"Me too."

His lips grazed the sides of her belly. "You know how I mentioned the other night at the coffee shop that there were *things* I wanted to tell you?"

His question was so unexpected, she opened

her eyes. *Talk about expectations being off-kilter.* The last thing she'd envisioned right now was conversation.

She opened her eyes to find him staring at her. "I remember."

He lifted himself away from her and lay down on his pillow again. "Essentially I told you only one of them."

"You sort of intimated a couple of other things in that one admission, like how you had to take over your mom's business…which made you very busy."

"Yeah." He hesitated. "But there were other… things."

With her life up in the air right now and too many complications from that warring for her head space, she wished they'd go back to pillow talk. "Did you rob a bank?"

He laughed. "No."

"Then why are you so glum? We're dynamite, heaven and fun all rolled into one. You should be savoring that."

"I like to be honest."

She liked that he was honest too. It was one of his best traits. As much as poetry and kisses, silliness and fun would have made things easier for her, she couldn't discourage that. "Okay."

"The other things aren't pretty."

She sat up and peered down at him. "I'm getting the feeling your last five years were very different from mine."

"I guess it all depends on your dating history."

She didn't think he'd been celibate for the past five years, but she had to admit she was curious enough to give him a few details of her own life, so he'd be comfortable giving her his.

"My dating history wasn't extensive. Three short relationships. A few dates scattered in between them."

"I had three longish relationships."

"Five whole years did pass."

"The first woman stole things from my house and sold them."

Once again, his comment was so far from what she expected that she couldn't control her reaction and she gasped. "What?"

"We had a miscommunication about her place in my life. In her mind, the things she took and sold were her attempt at balancing the power."

"She told you that?"

"I recognized it as her way of saying she got angry with me and sold things to buy herself something to make up for what she considered to be neglect."

Definitely someone who couldn't possibly be right for a serious guy like Jack. "That's...interesting."

"Honestly, that was easier to deal with than

girlfriend number two who cheated on me and girlfriend number three who burned down my beach house."

Her eyebrows rose so high she swore she lost them in her hairline. "Is this your way of telling me that you don't have good luck with women?"

"No. This is my way of telling you that I'm so busy I often forget things like dinner plans."

"I get that."

"Because you also work?"

"The other loves of your life didn't?"

He snorted at her reference to his girlfriends as loves of his life. "No."

"Well, no wonder number one stole from you. Unless she was an heiress, she probably needed money."

"She was a trust fund baby. She didn't need money. She needed attention. I never saw it." He reached up and stroked Autumn's face. "I don't want to hurt you again."

Ah. Now she understood. He wasn't exactly fishing to get her take on things. But he was trying to make sure they were on the same page with where they were going.

He held her gaze. "I'm committed to my company. Technically the first five years was the testing ground for the idea. The next five years will tell the tale of if the idea is strong enough that it can be replicated on a large scale in different markets and maintain a high level of success."

"I know you're busy. So am I. Raise Your Voice had only been in existence two years before I came on board. It's why I could wear so many hats and almost pick and choose my jobs. But in our infancy, I had to be a jack of all trades. Everybody did. We were always all-hands-on-deck. But as the charity got older and established itself, things settled down, our mission found its focus and we hired more people. Still, in those first few years I wouldn't have had time for a boyfriend."

"True."

"It also means, if I take over Gerry's job, I may want to look at reorganizing some things. I may want to find ways to improve services. Add services." She took a breath. "If Gerry really does retire—and his somewhat tipsy wife more or less confirmed he was considering it earlier tonight— I'll be as busy as you are. And I don't want to blow this chance. My mom could have never had a job outside the home. She threw herself into her family. She has the happiest husband and children on the face of the earth. So, I'm grateful. But it's not what I want. In my heart and soul, I am a businesswoman."

He rolled her to her back again. "So, we'll be like this wonderfully busy power couple who understand each other."

Relief poured through her. "Yes."

"We'll rule Manhattan."

She laughed. "I wouldn't go that far, but I will

tell you that we'll understand each other. We won't push for things that can't be. And maybe we'll both simply be happy for what we have."

He smiled. "I like that." He kissed her. "And I like this. And I like you."

"I like you too." The power of honesty surged through her again. But so did the power of being his equal. She wasn't her mom, the little woman who ran the household. Though she knew it took more skill and strength to be a stay-at-home mom than most people realized, she wasn't made to stay home. She was made to be in the workforce, negotiating, building, mentoring. He understood that.

She ran her toe down the back of his leg. "Remember that thing we did as soon as we got to my apartment five years ago?"

He chuckled. "How could I forget?"

"Let's do that."

CHAPTER ELEVEN

THEY WOKE THE next morning to the sound of his phone chirping. He groaned, rolled away from Autumn and answered with a groggy, "Hello?"

"Hey, Jack!"

"Sebastian, why aren't you on a honeymoon?"

"We leave Wednesday, remember?"

He ran his hand down his face. He'd had about thirty seconds of sleep. He was lucky he could remember his last name. "Sure."

"We're sitting here wondering where you are. You're supposed to come to the townhouse for the after-wedding brunch."

He sat up. Another brunch. At the townhouse. It had all been in Ivy's last memo to the bridal party. "I forgot."

"Don't worry. Looks like Autumn forgot too."

He nudged her with his foot, his eyes widening as he pointed at his phone to let her know they were in trouble or at the very least about to get caught spending the night together.

"Anyway, Ivy's going to call her now. We'll keep the blintzes warm for you."

With that he disconnected the call.

Jack had only time enough to say, "Ivy's about to call you," before her cell phone rang.

She sat up, her pale skin glowing in the morning sun that poured in through the wall of window facing east. "Hey, Ivy," she said, catching Jack's gaze. "Oh, darn. I slept in." She bit her lower lip and shook her head, as if embarrassed by the lie. But she had a look of devilment in her eyes.

"I'll get there as soon as I can."

She hung up the phone and looked at Jack. "How the heck am I going to get to a brunch when the only clothes I have are a bridesmaid's dress and heels that are way too high."

He leaned in and kissed her. A discussion about dresses and shoes was not the appropriate way to greet the woman who had rendered him speechless the night before. Holding her gaze, he pulled away and said, "Good morning."

She smiled. "Good morning. I don't suppose you have a size eight dress and seven and a half shoes in your closet?"

"No. But I have a neighbor about your size who might be willing to lend you a something."

"I'll take it."

He hit a speed dial number on his phone to ask Regina if she had anything Autumn could borrow. Then he called Arnie and asked to have the limo outside in fifteen minutes.

When he was done with his calls, she bounced out of bed and they headed for the shower. Luckily, they knew Arnie was on his way with the limo and Regina would soon drop by with a dress and shoes or the sight of her all soapy would have delayed their trip to Ivy and Sebastian's even more.

She got out first, towel dried and slipped into one of his robes as the elevator bell rang.

He leaned out of the all-glass shower. "That's probably Regina. I gave her today's code. She'll be standing in the entry when you get out there."

She saluted and ran off. He finished his shower and when he walked into the bedroom, she stood by the bed, wearing an ivory sweater dress and black high heels.

"Luckily, I had emergency lipstick and mascara in my purse."

He slid his hands around her from behind and kissed her hair. "Yes. Luckily."

She laughed and pushed him away. "If we want our arrival to be realistic, we need to arrive separately."

He took a regretful breath. "Okay. Fine."

She opened the little black evening bag she'd taken to the wedding to get a credit card and book a ride share on her phone.

He dressed in casual chinos and a sweater,

topped with a black leather jacket. They walked outside together, and her car awaited her. She got into the black SUV. He got into his limo.

Despite their efforts at concealment, they arrived at Ivy's simultaneously and walked up to the door together. When Sebastian opened it, he frowned.

"Her ride share pulled up the same time that Arnie and I did."

Sebastian said, "Convenient."

Jack smiled at Autumn. "Yeah. It was."

They ambled into the dining room behind Sebastian. Food warmed on the buffet on the back wall. Ivy's parents and Sebastian's parents sat at the dining room table talking. Plates pushed away and coffee cups brought forward, they'd obviously finished eating and were chatting.

"Where's everybody?"

"Not everybody showed up and of those who did most zipped off when they were done eating," Ivy said with a wince. "I got the impression lots of people are sick of us."

"Couldn't happen," Jack said, as Autumn said, "You did have a boatload of events."

"It's just so much easier sometimes to have everybody meet here," Ivy said petulantly.

Trying to appease her, Jack said, "The rehearsal dinner was nice."

Sebastian's parents said, "Thanks."

"And the wedding was even prettier," Autumn jumped in, seeing what Jack was trying to do. "Everything about this wedding was elegant and perfect," she said, taking a plate from the buffet and dishing out some eggs and breakfast potatoes.

Ivy laughed. "I loved your dance. You two were amazing."

"Jack had to look up the Charleston step on YouTube."

Everybody laughed.

"Hey. I might have had to do research, but I ended up doing a good job. And, admit it, you liked it."

"I loved it," Sebastian said. "Very manly."

"That's because Autumn told me to pretend that I was the extra-point kicker for the Giants."

The room fell silent as everyone thought that through, then a general rumble of laughter followed.

The tension of the room eased. While Jack and Autumn ate and Ivy and Sebastian's parents drank coffee and chitchatted, Ivy wound down. Sebastian relaxed on the seat at the end of the table.

At noon, Jack and Autumn left, forgetting to assume any kind of pretense that they weren't together. They reached the sidewalk where Arnie awaited, and Jack winced. "We forgot to get you a car." She pulled out her phone, but he stopped her with a hand over hers. "What if you didn't get a ride share?"

"You mean, let your driver take me to Queens?"

"I mean stay another night. It would be much easier to get to work tomorrow from my house than yours."

"Yeah."

She said it wistfully and he laughed. "You know you want to."

"I do. But you do realize that we'd have to run to my apartment now to pick up clothes for work and something that I can hang out in at your house today?"

"We could. Or we could call my personal shopper and ask her to pick up a few things."

She considered that. "Unless *we* did some shopping this afternoon?"

"Shopping?"

"I still have to get that sweater for my dad for Christmas."

He laughed as Arnie opened the limo door for them. "You know... I haven't been Christmas shopping in five years."

"Then it's time."

She climbed in and he slid in beside her. Arnie closed the door. Jack swore he felt the earth shift, as if something significant had happened.

But it hadn't. It couldn't.

He'd learned his lesson about relationships. He was no good at them. Mostly because he had nothing left to offer at the end of the day.

And Autumn didn't want a relationship. If her boss retired and she was promoted, she'd be as busy as he was—

Technically, they were the perfect couple.

He frowned. *Maybe something profound had happened?*

He'd found someone as busy as he was, who wanted what he did.

Why did that suddenly make him feel uneasy?

Arnie dropped them off at the entry to Macy's. The place was decorated to the nines with a dramatic Christmas tree on the back wall of the mezzanine above them. Covered in blue lights, it dominated the space. Evergreen branches were everywhere, highlighted with lights, colorful ornaments or pinecones.

He glanced around like an alien on a new planet. He hadn't been shopping in forever and the whole experience of the store amazed him.

Autumn had no such problem. She led him to the women's department, quickly chose a dress for work the next day, yoga pants and a big T-shirt for hanging out and some undergarments. They walked out and Arnie drove them back to the penthouse.

But when they stepped inside the lobby, he

noticed the ornate decorations of his admittedly fancy building. Silver tinsel framed the huge windows facing the street. Small red bells looped across the front of the lobby desk. A silver tree decorated with oversize red ornaments sat in the corner. Candles with evergreen branches as bases adorned tables and the credenza leading to the elevators.

He looked at it all, his head turning right and left as he and Autumn made their way to the private elevator that would take them to his penthouse.

"You act like you haven't seen Christmas decorations before."

He didn't want to admit he hadn't paid any attention since his mom died, but her comment hung in the air, leaving him no choice.

"Truth is I hadn't really noticed Christmas decorations the past few years. But the decorations in Macy's were so eye-popping I couldn't help seeing them and they sort of opened my eyes to decorations everywhere."

"You've been hit by the Christmas bug."

He laughed. "There is no such thing as a Christmas bug."

"Sure, there is. It's like the flu except instead of wanting to spend the day in bed until you feel better, you want to spend the day looking at Christmas decorations and be around happy shoppers."

"I have never in my life wanted to be around a happy shopper." He caught her gaze as he carried her packages back to the main bedroom. "I'm not even convinced shoppers are happy. They all looked intense and driven to me."

"That's the look of a person trying to get the right gift."

"Much easier to use a personal shopper."

She shook her head, rummaged through her bags until she found the yoga pants and T-shirt and slipped off Regina's dress. He stared at her, his mouth watering. After all the things they'd done the night before, he shouldn't have the desperate urge that whooshed through him. But he did.

Too soon she slid the T-shirt over her head and jumped into the yoga pants.

"What do you want to do now?"

He wanted to go back to bed. But that sounded a little heavy handed. Besides, after the morning with Ivy and Sebastian and an afternoon of shopping he probably should feed her. "We could order dinner and watch a movie. Or if you're not hungry yet, we could watch a movie and order dinner after."

"How long will it take for dinner to get here?"

"Depends on what we order. Steak from Gallaghers would probably take an hour because they generally get busy. Pizza could be here in twenty minutes."

"I'm hungry enough to wait for a steak."

He smiled. "Yeah. Me too."

They ordered, watched a movie, eating the steak and French fries when they eventually arrived. He found another movie for them, but she began to yawn.

"Neither one of us had much sleep last night. So rather than tough it out, what do you say we go to bed?"

She yawned again. "Good idea."

Getting ready for bed, exhaustion began to claim him too. Still, once they crawled under the covers, they gravitated like a magnet and steel and fell into bliss.

She drifted off to sleep first and he settled on his pillow. But instead of sleep, an odd feeling of doom filled him. He knew it was because the last time he and Autumn were together terrible things had happened. He told himself to forget their first night, his mom's heart attack and being overwhelmed with work. But even after he drifted off, the sensation invaded his dreams in the form of reminders of the failures and difficulties of the past five years.

He woke almost as tired as when he went to sleep, with the command running through his head that he couldn't get comfortable with this thing he and Autumn were doing. He couldn't get passive. He couldn't let it run them. He had to keep control of this so neither of them got hurt.

Autumn awakened in Jack's bed, though he was nowhere around. She took a second to listen and realized he was in the shower. Naked and happy, she rolled out of bed. After laying out her new work dress, she made her way into the bathroom. Jack was toweling off, but he paused long enough to give her a good morning kiss.

She got into the shower as he left the bathroom to dress.

She should have felt odd. At the very least uncomfortable. They'd known each other a couple of weeks, but they were comfortable naked, comfortable living together.

In fact, her heart slipped a notch when she thought about going home that night. Not because she liked his gorgeous penthouse. Because home was empty. He was here.

If that wasn't a red flag that she was getting in too deep, Autumn didn't know what was. Which meant she was going to have to go home after work that night. She couldn't let things get serious.

She took her time drying her hair and styling it. When she came out of the bathroom, he was nowhere around. But she smelled toast. She slipped into her dress and found him in the kitchen. White cabinets surrounded a huge island with Carrara marble countertops. She pulled out one of the tall stools with black wrought iron backs.

"Toast?"

She sat on the stool. "I'd love some."

"Coffee is there," he said, pointing at a one-cup brewer.

She got off the stool and headed over. "Can I make you a cup?"

He pointed at a half-filled mug by the toaster.

Her fears that they were getting in too deep dissolved into nothing because it appeared things weren't so perfect between them after all. Her heart jerked. Would this have been what it would be like if he'd stayed with her the night of their one-night stand?

Awkward? Silent? That just-get-out-of-here feeling in the air?

He set a small plate containing two pieces of toast in front of her. "Can Arnie and I drop you off at work?"

"I can easily get there from here."

He turned back to the toaster. "Okay."

She ate her toast in silence as he read his phone. Then they went their separate ways.

She tried to be chipper and happy at work, answering everyone's questions and even accepting

Gerry's apology when he called her into his office to explain that his wife didn't get out much.

"Well, she certainly intends to fix that when you retire," Autumn replied with a laugh.

He squirmed in his chair. "Yes. About that. I wasn't going to announce until the first of the year but since my wife let the cat out of the bag, I'll be announcing my retirement at tonight's board meeting."

Her heart perked up. "That's…great? I mean, is this what you want?"

"Absolutely. We've been vacationing in Sarasota for years. It's where we want to be."

"Then congratulations!"

"My early announcement means everything will speed up. I'll start interviewing candidates now and probably the board will have someone chosen before the first of the year."

"Oh."

He frowned.

New confident Autumn couldn't stay silent. "I didn't think you'd need to interview." She almost wimped out and stopped with that statement but forced herself to move forward. "I thought I'd replace you."

"You might," he agreed, shifting on his chair again.

"Is there something wrong? Something that makes you think I wouldn't be a good replacement."

He took a breath. "It's not that. Exactly." He winced. "Seriously, you're so tight with Ivy, a board member and major contributor, that nobody's really looked at what you were doing in years."

"I was doing a lot!"

"Of course. And if you apply for the job, you'll have plenty of opportunity to show us all that."

Her heart sunk with disappointment—not that she should have been a shoo-in for the job, and no one noticed, but that no one seemed to have recognized everything she did. Still, she put her shoulders back and decided to take charge of getting the position she wanted.

The only problem was, she wasn't sure how. She'd done mountains of work, solved problems, helped clients…and no one had seen.

Plus, she'd already had one shot at impressing Gerry and, obviously, she'd failed or this conversation would have gone very differently.

She rose. "Thank you for letting me know."

"You're welcome." He smiled at her. "And if you really believe you're a good candidate for the job, I look forward to getting your resume and giving you a chance to interview."

CHAPTER TWELVE

JACK DIDN'T RETURN from work until after eight that night. That fact alone told him that he was correct in keeping things simple with Autumn. He set his takeout dinner on the big island, grabbed utensils from a drawer and settled in the living room to eat.

He turned on that night's basketball game as he ate his chef's salad, but neither held his attention. The entire penthouse seemed cold and dead. The day had been too long. After weeks of Autumn popping in and out of his life, damn it, he was bored.

He picked up his phone. She answered on the third ring.

"What are you doing?"

"Don't you mean what are you wearing?"

He laughed. "This isn't an obscene phone call." But the exhaustion of the day fell away.

"Too bad. I'm on the subway. I'm bored."

"Still on the subway?"

"Stayed late."

"Lots to catch up on after the wedding?"

There was a pause. A long one. Finally, he said, "Autumn?"

"My boss told me today he's retiring. I must have been under consideration to replace him because he took me to dinner and asked me questions about my job. But I don't think I passed muster."

He settled in on the sofa. "That's ridiculous."

"Not really. He already told me no one knew what I did, but he also mentioned my friendship with Ivy…as if being her friend made me untouchable and they couldn't have that."

"That's a tad insulting to both you and Ivy."

"He told me I could apply for the job. I'd have to interview, etc."

"Which is the perfect opportunity to prove your worth."

She went silent again. Jack waited. Finally, he said, "But you don't want to."

"I wish. The real problem is I don't think I know how. I've worked my ass off for these people for seven long years and no one noticed me?"

"No. No one gave you credit for what you did. Do you have a team that works for you?"

"I have a couple of assistants I delegate to—"

"Do you think one of them might have been taking credit for your work or ideas?"

"I don't know. I can't seem to analyze this situation properly. I never thought I'd have to apply for this job and the comments about my relationship with Ivy just add to the confusion."

"I think the real bottom line is that you didn't make sure your superiors saw what you were doing."

She said nothing.

"Autumn?"

She took a breath then glanced at him. "I don't like to brag."

"There's a difference between bragging and taking credit." And she didn't seem to know that, almost as if there was something holding her back.

"How about this? How about if you bring your resume to the penthouse tomorrow and let me look at it?"

"My resume?"

"We'll tackle this together. Since your resume is the first thing they'll see. That's where we'll start."

"Okay. But the only resume I have is the one I got this job with. I haven't updated it."

"That's okay. Starting from scratch gives us a good opportunity to write something strong. You want your resume to speak for you. You want it to demonstrate your worth. It's your first opportunity to show them your worth."

Her voice brightened. "Right. That's true."

"How does a person who works at an agency that helps women rise through the ranks of corporate America not know this?"

"I planned events, talked to the press, monitored the office, found mentors, assigned clients to them. I never actually *was* a mentor."

"Oh. Okay."

She sighed. "You could have knocked me over with a feather when Gerry told me he didn't know what I did, then criticized my relationship with Ivy. I always believed I knew the system. Now, I'm beginning to see what a lot of our clients go through. It was like a punch in the gut to realize I wasn't a shoo-in for the position. Which is exactly what our clients encounter in their day jobs when they're passed over for promotions. I'm as shellshocked as I'll bet most of them are."

"You do realize that after you go through the process to get that job, you'll be the perfect candidate to run the organization that helps them."

"I guess I could look at this as a good thing."

He smiled. "A learning experience. You will be going through what your clients go through every day…and what better person to guide the organization created to help them than someone who knows their struggle?"

"Yes."

He heard the strength return to her voice and pride expanded his chest. He liked that they were friends and that she didn't hesitate to let him assist her. There wasn't any doubt in his mind that she would get the job. She simply needed to see that for herself and expand the confidence she would get when they ran through mock interviews.

Which meant their spending time together had purpose—

Her coming to his penthouse the following night wouldn't be about them inching toward a relationship that couldn't happen. She needed a boost and an objective opinion, and he could provide it.

So, their getting together wasn't about expanding their relationship.

But that didn't mean they couldn't have some fun.

His voice casual and logical, he said, "Bring clothes and stay over. That way you won't have a subway ride home or to work the next morning."

She laughed. "So, I'm sleeping in the guest-room?"

"Not hardly." Because she couldn't see him, he rolled his eyes at her silliness. "Arnie and I will pick you up about six."

"I might have to stay late—"

"No. Your work now is getting that CEO job. That's where your focus should be."

When she stepped out of the office Tuesday evening at six, the limo awaited her. Jack exited the backseat and held the door for her. She slid inside and he slid in behind her, caught her shoulders, turned her to him and kissed her.

"Hey."

"Hey." Their gazes locked and all the weird feelings she'd had that day disappeared. Not merely the confusing bubble of excitement over seeing him again, but the billion things that popped up all day. Especially wondering how anybody could have missed the level of work she did. She didn't want to be angry...but damn it, how could she not be? The comments about Ivy, as if Ivy had gotten her her job and helped her keep it, were infuriating.

Still, deep down inside she worried that this was her fault. Her parents had always been so focused on her brothers' success, downplaying anything she did, that she'd become accustomed to staying in the background.

Was she actually downplaying her part in the charity's success because she was afraid of success...or afraid she didn't deserve it?

She didn't know, but she did recognize she had to grow beyond any feelings of self-doubt she had because her parents hadn't seen her as a business-person, the way they had her brothers.

"Thanks for helping me. I'm starting to think I don't know how to take credit for what I've done."

He laughed. "I'm happy to help you see the light."

"I'm serious. This might sound horribly old fashioned, but my parents worked very hard to assure my brothers were educated enough that they could conquer the world if they wanted to. They helped me as much with tuition as they did my brothers, but they motivated my brothers more." She shook her head. "I know it sounds crazy, but I think I might have ended up believing I didn't deserve the career they did."

When she said it out loud, there was no might about it. She'd fought her whole life against becoming a "little woman" the way her mom had been. But she'd never anticipated the subtle damage that had occurred because her parents didn't see her as an equal.

Yet here it was. She'd downplayed her accomplishments. Hadn't sought recognition.

"Those are easy fixes."

Doubt tried to overwhelm her, but she fought it. "I hope so."

They drove to the penthouse and she changed into the sweats and T-shirt she'd brought. When she came out of the bedroom, he was by the stove. Something sizzled in a frying pan.

She sniffed the air. "Oh, man. Whatever that is, it smells great."

"It's the makings of Step Inside's famous fajitas."

"I've had those!"

"Everyone has. This was one of the recipes I created when Mom opened her first restaurant."

Resume in hand, she slid on the stool.

"It's been hacked and put on the internet."

She gasped, but he laughed. "Imitation is the greatest form of flattery."

He motioned to the resume. "Start with your education and move to the job history."

"I don't have much of a job history. I've been at Raise Your Voice since graduating university."

"Then we're going to have to make sure that you highlight everything, and I mean every darned thing you do for the company. Because your accounting experience is limited, we'll have to make sure we set out the classes you had at university and what you learned."

He motioned again for her to read and turned to stir the sizzling fajita makings.

She read her education, which basically said the school she attended and when she graduated. Sliding the fajita makings from pan to platter, he said, "You need to beef that up by listing important classes—especially the accounting courses. When you wrote this, you were applying for an assistant's job. Now you want to run the place. Even if it seems like overkill, you have to list the things that demonstrate that you have the knowledge to do that."

He talked as he warmed the tortillas and filled

them with steak, peppers, onion and avocado and she made copious notes. Then he told her to put away the resume and join him in front of the television to eat the fajitas.

He picked up the remote. She picked up her fajita. She expected the TV to spring on. Instead, he stood watching her, waiting for her reaction to her first bite.

She groaned. "Oh, my gosh! That's good."

He grinned. "I know." He sat beside her on the sofa and turned on a basketball game. "Someday, I'm going to make you an omelet."

"Lucky me."

"You are lucky. And so are the Pistons. Have you ever seen them have a year like this?"

"No. But I don't watch basketball as much as I used to before I started working."

He peered over. "Do you like it?"

She shrugged. "I love basketball. I'm on the subway when the games start. I mostly see the second half."

"I have season tickets. Rarely use them."

She gaped at him. "Oh, that ends now."

He laughed. "I usually give the tickets to vendors, employees I want to reward or friends. But if you'd like to be courtside—"

Her eyes widened. "Courtside?"

"Yelling at refs, cheering for the Knicks, I suppose we could arrange it."

She set down her fajita, twisted to face him and kissed him. Her simple thanks turned into something hot and spicy and they did things on his sofa that made them both breathless.

Their fajitas were cold before they got back to them, but neither cared and the next night they were courtside, watching the Knicks, yelling at refs and cheering on players.

She finished her resume on Thursday and turned it in to Gerry, who smiled and said, "Thanks."

She didn't know how a person could convey coolness in one word, but Gerry pulled it off, zapping her confidence enough that she called Jack.

"He didn't seem thrilled when I gave him my resume."

In his office, looking over yet another draft of the new five-year plan his financial staff had given him, Jack leaned back in his chair. Autumn needing assistance coupled with their mutual love of the Knicks had balanced out their relationship. It wasn't just romance and hearts and flowers and sleeping together. They were becoming friends.

Those were good reasons to continue to be involved. Casual reasons. Nothing serious happening between them.

"I think that means we're going to have to practice your interview skills."

She sighed. "Really?"

"Hey, it's not a big deal. I'll ask you a few questions and then tell you if any red flags pop up in your answers."

"Red flags?"

"Things that make boards of directors cringe. When you become CEO, the Raise Your Voice board becomes your boss. You have to know how to deal with people who will be criticizing your performance and your ideas. If you get huffy or say something that makes you seem difficult, they won't promote you."

"I'm never huffy or arrogant."

"Let me be the judge of that." He waited a second, then said, "You didn't happen to bring extra clothes to work, did you?"

"I have those spare yoga pants I used for our dance lessons."

"Let me call my personal shopper and get you something to wear to work tomorrow. That way we can go over your interview skills tonight."

"Tonight?"

"Yes. This is too important to leave to chance. Plus, because you work in that office, I worry that Gerry will call you in for an impromptu interview and you won't be ready."

"Impromptu interview?"

"Just trying to cover all the bases. He asked you to dinner to question you about your job and never

gave you a hint that was coming. It wouldn't surprise me if he didn't just call you into his office
someday and start asking interview questions."

"We do tend to lean toward a more casual office."

He relaxed. "Okay. We'll prep you tonight
and he can call you into his office tomorrow and
you'll be ready."

She laughed. "You bet I will."

"That's the spirit. Size eight on the dress,
right?"

"Yes."

"Okay, Arnie and I will pick you up at six."

CHAPTER THIRTEEN

NOT MORE THAN five seconds after Autumn disconnected the call from Jack, her phone rang with a call from her mother.

"Hey, Ma. What's up?"

"I just wanted to tell you how much we enjoyed the wedding."

She leaned back, relaxing in her chair. "It was beautiful."

"And everyone was so friendly."

"Ivy and Sebastian both have lovely families."

"We spent the longest time talking with your friend Jack."

That made her sit up again. He'd said he'd spoken with her parents, but her mom made it sound like a marathon session. She very carefully said, "He's a nice guy."

"Very nice. Do you know he owns Step Inside?"

"Yes."

"He was a chef."

"I know."

"And now he runs the place. Just like your brother Aaron."

"Aaron's not a chef."

"No. But he started off as an entry-level accountant and now he runs the investment firm."

Excitement over interviewing for the CEO position coupled with hating the way her mom bragged about her brothers and before she knew it, she said, "I might someday run *this* place."

"Raise Your Voice?"

The confusion in her mom's tone boosted the sense that it was time to come clean with her mom and admit she had ambitions. Up until this point it had been easy to pretend she was an average office worker. But with Gerry retiring and a potential new job on the horizon, it seemed right to get this out in the open.

"Yes. My boss made it official that he's retiring. I've been supervising most of the general work of the charity for years. I know more about what goes on here than anyone."

Even as she said the words, she felt her confidence building. To hell with Gerry's skepticism. She could do this, and she would wow that board of directors when it came time to interview with them.

She simply had to wow Gerry first. Jack's coaching would make that possible.

"I'll be interviewing for the job before the end of the year."

"Well, that's lovely," her mom said slowly as if she'd never considered the fact that her daughter might make something of herself. "But don't you want to get married and have kids?"

"You chose to devote your life to your family," Autumn said, not getting upset about the question because she knew her mom's opinions were the result of living a different kind of life, having different goals and purposes. Still, this wasn't the time to have the discussion about *her* choices. That would only lead to an argument or a sermon. She wasn't in the mood for either.

Being deliberately vague, she said, "There are other ways to live."

"Sure. But having kids and running a company would be difficult."

"I'm a strong person," she said, steering clear of a real answer again, though her relationship with Jack popped into her brain. Neither of them was commitment oriented. Both wanted to be the best they could be in their careers. That's why their arrangement would work.

"Yes, you are a strong person, Autumn. You always have been a strong person. And you march to your own drummer."

Autumn cringed, but she recognized her mom meant that as a compliment.

"I also know," her mom continued, "that if you set your mind to do something, you will. And I'm proud of you."

The unexpected praise almost stopped her breathing. "Thanks, Ma."

"You're welcome. Now, the second reason I called was to remind you that I'd love to have you come to the house on Christmas Eve and Christmas Day, but both of your brothers bowed out until Christmas Day. Both said something about visiting in-laws on Christmas Eve." She sighed. "This is what happens when someone gets married. There are two families to accommodate."

"True," she said, biting the inside of her lip, suddenly confused. Maybe it was the talk of her brothers and their in-laws, but she realized she and Jack hadn't talked about the holiday. And she almost didn't think it would be appropriate to bring it up. If he said he had plans, that could get awkward. If he said he didn't but didn't want her around, that could be worse. Both of which meant it was too early to make an issue of it. If he said something, good. If he didn't…she'd be fine.

"Anyway, that means we'll just be doing Christmas Day. Also, you can bring your friend, Jack. Your dad and I like him."

It might be too soon for her to make an issue of it, but it was never too soon for her mother to matchmake.

"He was my partner for the wedding. He wasn't my date."

"Yeah, but he is a nice guy. It would be okay to invite him for dinner."

She squeezed her eyes shut, thinking this through, trying to come up with the response that would stop her mom before she got on a roll.

Her mom sighed. "If there's a reason *you* don't want to invite him, *I* can call him…"

She blanched. Not only would it be weird for her mom to call Jack, but there were eight million ways Jack could misinterpret that kind of call from her mother.

Oh, Lord. Even after all their discussions about not wanting a commitment, her mom could make her look like a bride on the auction block.

There was only one way to handle this. "Okay. If you want me to call him, I will." She'd never talk her mom out of inviting him, so at least if she asked Jack if he wanted to come to dinner, she could control the narrative. "The thing is, just because he and I were partners in a wedding, that doesn't make us friends. If he chooses to come to dinner it will be as *your* friend. Not mine."

"You don't like him?"

She adored him. He was smart, funny and whimsical. But his coming to her parents' home for Christmas dinner wasn't part of their deal. "He's a very nice person. But I can read between the lines. *You* like him and *you* think he'd be a good match for me. If you try to make something happen between us, it will be embarrassing for all of us and ruin Christmas dinner."

Her mom said, "Mmm. Okay. I get it. But he can still come for dinner."

"As *your* friend?"

"Sure. Ask Jack to come to dinner as *my* friend."

After a few more comments about gifts, Autumn disconnected the call shaking her head. If Jack came to Christmas dinner, even if she explained it was because her parents liked him—not an invitation from her—it was going to be awkward. Complicated. Especially if he accepted the invitation and her mom went against her word and tried to matchmake.

She would literally have to warn him that matchmaking was a possibility. Then at dinner, they'd have to pretend they weren't already in a romantic relationship.

And exactly how would that work?

Would they feign a growing interest in each other as dinner went on to keep her mom happy?

Or should they pretend disinterest in each other so her mother would back off?

It seemed…too complicated.

And embarrassing.

And wrong.

Not in their deal.

She lowered her forehead to her computer. Now she remembered why her mom never met any of her boyfriends.

Jack's limo pulled up to the building housing the offices for Raise Your Voice and Autumn came racing out. She slid into the backseat but didn't give him a chance to kiss her hello before she said, "My mom wants you to come to Christmas dinner."

Tired from a long day of work, he wasn't sure he'd heard that right. "What?"

"My mom called me today. She and dad love you. They want you to come to Christmas dinner."

"Because they like me?"

She winced. "Yes and no. They like you but I'm pretty sure my mom is matchmaking. The bottom line is they like you enough to think you're good for me."

He considered that. "That's a compliment, right?"

"Yes. I'm sorry. It *is* a compliment. But it's also confusing. I don't want my parents to get the wrong idea about us. Meaning, the dinner will be complicated."

The stab of disappointment he got when she said she didn't want her parents to get the wrong idea about them surprised him. Still, he saw her point. It would be weird to be at a matchmaking dinner when they already sort of were a match, but not really, and they didn't want anyone to know they were seeing each other.

He couldn't remember when they'd decided that, except they'd pretended they weren't a couple with Ivy and Sebastian the day after their wedding. He supposed they'd set that trend right then and there.

A family dinner with her would also set a precedent.

It almost seemed smarter to come clean and admit things—

Except, they didn't even know what they were doing together. How could they explain it to her family? Her *parents*?

"Give them my regrets and apologies. Say I have a prior commitment."

She met his gaze. "Do you?"

He glanced out the window and saw the happy red and green lights that shimmered in the falling snow. Reminders of Christmases with his mom flitted through his brain. She'd had so many friends that there wasn't a Christmas that wasn't filled with entertaining. He'd cooked. She'd schmoozed. Wine and laughter had flowed like water.

He hadn't missed that until now...because shopping with Autumn had reminded him that he hadn't noticed Christmas for five years. Now he couldn't seem to stop noticing it.

Realizing she was waiting for his answer, he smiled and said, "It's a big city. I always find something to do."

The way her eyes shifted told him she was remembering that his mom had passed, and he was an only child. He hadn't mentioned not having other relatives, but he supposed he didn't have to.

He slid across the seat and put his arm around her, changing the mood by changing the subject. "I've thought of a hundred really good interview questions to ask you tonight when we practice for your big day."

"Really?"

"Yes. And I'm going to cook for you again."

That made her smile. "That sounds promising."

"I thought I'd make something simple tonight. Chicken, sweet potatoes and garlic green beans."

The limo stopped in front of his building as she said, "Yum."

He opened the back door. "I'm using food to make you comfortable as I grill you. It will be like a mental anchor. When you think of interviewing, you'll be reminded of eating my delicious dinner and instantly be in a good mood. Which will make you positive and upbeat with Gerry."

They exited the limo and she cuddled against him as they entered the lobby. "I'll take it."

He kissed her cheek and they walked toward the elevator, Christmas decorations blinking at him, as if they had to work to get his attention. They didn't. Since his mom died, he hadn't felt alone on Christmas. He'd ignored the holiday. Why his subconscious suddenly wanted to be part of it again, he had no idea. But he couldn't it shake it off.

As he prepared the sweet potatoes to go into the oven, she pulled up the notepad app on her phone and sat at the center island. When she was settled, he didn't waste a minute and began asking interview questions.

"You've been working for us for over five years, but no one seems to know what you do... Can you explain that?"

She smiled craftily. "I've actually thought about this question and I realized no one understands what I do because I'm good at my job."

He shook his head. "Be careful. There's a thin line between confidence and arrogance."

She nodded, made a note in her phone, then looked up and tried her answer again. "I've actually thought about this question and I realized no one understands what I do because I work independently. I've been with Raise Your Voice almost from its inception. Back then, everybody pitched in and helped with everything. There were no job descriptions, but we all found our niches. I gravitated toward event planning and public relations, but I also love working with mentors. Those three jobs more or less became mine.

Having done them for so long I don't often have questions or need assistance. The broad scope of my duties also gives me a very good feel for the organization. I know the mentors. I can handle the media. I understand our mission."

"I don't see any accounting in your background."

"I took courses at university. I can read and interpret reports made by the accounting department. In my current position, I also set budgets and meet them."

The questions went on like that as the sweet potatoes baked and the chicken grilled.

They paused long enough to set the island with dishes and utensils and even begin eating. Then the questions started again.

Amazed at her knowledge, Jack couldn't find a way to stump her. She really did know almost everything about Raise Your Voice. She'd lived through most of the history of the charity. She could speak with authority about the Raise Your Voice mission, but also their mistakes. Their learning experiences.

When they were done, he stared at her in awe. "There's a part of me that wonders if you don't know more than your current CEO does, if only because you have this ridiculous ability to remember details."

She laughed. "I think it's all about loving the charity."

With the dishes in the dishwasher, they plopped down on the sofa. "I think you're right. Nothing serves a company better than a leader who loves the company's mission."

"Is that the secret to your success?"

"Yes and no. I know food. I know people. I know how much people like to get together over a good meal. So, I work to assure that our meals are festive and happy."

"From behind a desk?"

"When my mom first started Step Inside, I was the chef. I created our menu. I was supposed to form a whole new division of research and development to ensure our menu was always top of the line." He shrugged. "My being in touch with that end of things is like you understanding how a good event doesn't merely raise money, it raises awareness of your charity's mission."

She nodded, then nestled against his side as they watched a movie. They showered together, laughing and playing, making love under the shower spray before climbing into bed and discovering new and more interesting ways to tease and pleasure each other.

The next morning, he made her an omelet for breakfast and the kiss of thanks she gave him when he dropped her off at the building housing Raise Your Voice almost had him dragging her back to his penthouse to spend the morning in bed.

But he didn't. They both had jobs. They were a power couple. That's what he liked.

Still, he couldn't keep himself from calling her at noon. She no longer seemed surprised by his calls, and he loved hearing the smile in her voice when she said hello.

But when she sighed and told him she'd mentioned to her mom that he was unavailable for Christmas, he got a funny tweak in his heart.

"She's disappointed. She said Daddy will be too. But she certainly understood."

He remembered talking to her parents at the wedding, sitting at their table, feeling at home, drinking a beer with her dad.

They were nice people. Salt of the earth people, his mother would have called them. If he wasn't trying to hide his affair with their daughter, he might have actually taken them up on their invitation.

Which would only complicate things.

He had to remember that. What he and Autumn had was perfect. He did not want to ruin it.

CHAPTER FOURTEEN

FRIDAY NIGHT AFTER WORK, they drove to Queens. He went inside with her while she gathered clothes—including one of the gowns she wore to Raise Your Voice events because he had a Christmas ball to attend and had invited her to join him.

As she packed, he walked around the living space. The kitchen and dining room were combined, but the living room was large enough to accommodate a sectional sofa and oversize chair with an upholstered ottoman. The place was exactly as he remembered. Same furniture. Clean in a way only a single person could accomplish. The faint scent of lavender wafting through the air.

He waited for sadness to settle over him. When it didn't, he decided enough time had passed that he'd disassociated Autumn and his tragedy, but he also realized he'd barely known her the first time he'd been here. Now, they'd spent a couple of weeks together. His only connection to her wasn't a one-night stand. It was more like a friendship that had nothing to do with that one-night stand.

Satisfied with that explanation, he smiled as she walked out of the bedroom and said, "Ready?"

He took the bag from her hand. "Yes." He gave her a quick kiss. "Should be a very fun weekend."

Arnie drove them back to Manhattan. They ate at a cute Italian restaurant near his building, then they walked home through the falling snow.

Saturday afternoon, he asked her a few interview questions, but he was in the mood for lunch out, and they went to the first Step Inside restaurant.

She smiled when they entered. "So pretty. Christmas with a twist. Like Ivy's wedding reception."

"We let every manager decorate their own store." He looked around at the aqua and purple decor and decided he liked it. "We also have a contest. Every employee of the restaurant with the best decorations gets an extra week of vacation."

She turned to him with wide eyes. "Wow. That's incentive!"

"A little something to remember when you're the boss."

Knowing they had an event that evening that included dinner, they ordered only tomato soup and toasted cheese sandwiches. She groaned with pleasure over her sandwich.

"The secret is just a hint of chili powder."

She gaped at him. "Seriously?"

"It goes well with tomato soup."

A weird feeling shuffled through him. The way he kept slipping into chef mode confused him. Of course, Autumn loved his cooking and seemed to love his tidbits of information—

He had to be making too much out of nothing.

They strolled through Central Park in the falling snow, and when they returned to the penthouse it was time to dress for the ball.

A couple hours later, he was in his tux in the living room, watching college football, waiting for her. When she came out of the bedroom, his heart skipped a beat. Wearing a sparkly red gown, with her hair pinned up and dangling earrings that highlighted her long, slender neck, she stole his breath.

He slowly rose from the sofa. "You look amazing."

She walked over and straightened the bow tie, then the lapel of his tux. "You do too." She rose to her tiptoes to kiss him. "Some men were made to wear a tux and you are definitely one of them."

Her praise filled him with pleasure, but as quickly as she realized it, the odd sensation he kept getting all day prickled along his nerve endings. He wasn't the kind of person who needed accolades or compliments. He supposed it was the fact that the praise was from *her* that made it noteworthy.

But it confused him. He didn't behave like this. Usually, he was more disinterested. Almost like more of an observer of life than someone living—

He nearly rolled his eyes at his thoughts. Who cared if he was pleased that she thought he was handsome? It actually worked very well for two people involved romantically. And it was nothing more than that.

They drove to the Waldorf and checked their coats before taking their place in the receiving line.

Autumn had attended her share of charity balls, but there was something about this ball that filled her with awe. The size and scope alone were mindboggling. But the decorations and atmosphere were almost hypnotic.

"I don't know who your friend's party planner is, but…wow…" She glanced around at silver and gold decorations, fine china trimmed in gold on blindingly white linen tablecloths and candy cane lilies in arrangements for centerpieces. All of which were accented by red and silver lights that alternated around the room.

"This is lovely."

"Yeah."

He said it calmly, as if the hundred round tables set up around a turntable bar was something he saw every day, and she suddenly realized he might be accustomed this kind of ball. He might not go to one every week or even every month. But he'd been to his fair share—

Meaning, she'd stepped out of her world and into his. Her breath stuttered at the thought. She might plan high class events, but not this big. Her guests might be the cream of the crop in the city, but this party reached another level. Movie stars casually milled about. Two tech geniuses headquartered on the West Coast chatted by the bar. She swore she saw a prince and two Middle Eastern kings.

They reached the hosts, and Jack introduced her to Paul and Tilly Montgomery. At least eighty, with silver hair set off by a blue gown, Tilly took Autumn's hands in both of hers.

"Oh, my dear, how lovely to see our Jack has finally brought a woman to one of my parties."

Afraid Jack might have been insulted, Autumn hid a wince. "Thank you… I think."

Tilly chortled. "Seriously, Jack. You might have actually found a keeper this time."

Jack leaned in and kissed Tilly's cheek. "I'm still waiting for you."

Her husband, Paul, sighed. "I'm standing right here, Jack. If you're going to flirt with my wife at least have the good graces to do it behind my back."

Jack shook his hand, his face blossoming with

fondness for the older couple. "I want you to be aware that your wife has options, so you step up your game."

Chuckling, Paul slapped his back. "It's good to see you happy again, kid."

Jack said, "I'm always happy."

Tilly and Paul exchanged a look that Autumn saw. They truly liked seeing Jack happy. And they didn't for one minute buy his claim that he was always happy.

Jack put his hand on the small of her back and led her into the ballroom, but Tilly's and Paul's comments stayed with her. They liked Jack and loved that he was happy—

She made him happy.

Or their arrangement did.

A waiter walked by with champagne and Jack plucked two glasses and handed one to her.

"Thank you."

"We don't have to stay long."

"Are you kidding?" Maybe she was a little high on the power she seemed to have to make Jack happy, but there was no way she wanted to leave. "This room is gorgeous. There's a band. And movie stars!"

"And here I thought you were happy to be with me."

She leaned in and kissed him. "You're the icing on the cake."

He laughed.

"You know I love being with you." Remembering how it felt to realize she made Jack happy, she said, "You make me happy. I always have fun with you."

He smiled as if he didn't have a care in the world, but Tilly's and Paul's comments came back to her. He might be the Jack she remembered from five years ago. Fun, easygoing. But Tilly and Paul had seen another side of him. They'd seen him grieving his mom. They'd seen him alone. They might have also seen him after his fiancées stole his ability to trust.

No wonder Tilly and Paul were pleased to see him happy.

A couple greeted Jack and stopped to wish him a merry Christmas. He turned to Autumn and said, "Tom, Grace, this is Autumn Jones. You might remember her from her work with Raise Your Voice. Autumn, this is Tom and Grace Howell. Tom's on my board of directors."

Autumn shook hands and said, "It's nice to meet you," as the strange feeling rippled through her again. But this time she recognized it. She might have stepped out of her world and into his, but she fit. She didn't feel out of place. She belonged at Jack's side. Not as arm candy, but as herself. She made him happy. She *loved* making him happy.

And he made her happy.

Seated with a group of Jack's friends, they enjoyed lively conversation at dinner. After dessert, Tilly walked up to the microphone and said a few words thanking everyone for coming and encouraging them to celebrate the season with her. Then the band began to play, and she and Jack took to the floor.

Just two short weeks ago, they'd been muddling through dance lessons with Greg, awkward with each other. Now, they fit in each other's arms, laughed when he swung her around, and enjoyed the night.

Then they were taken home in the limo she'd gotten very accustomed to.

When they arrived in his penthouse, he took her into his arms again, this time to kiss her. He looked her in the eye with his beautiful blue orbs and the horrible truth hit her. She didn't merely fit into his world. She loved him.

Again.

This time when he slipped off her gown and she undid the buttons of his shirt there was a familiarity that opened her heart like a blossom in the sun. Touching him took new meaning. Their connection breathed life into her soul. When she kissed him, she wanted him to know that. She wanted him to realize how special he was.

His kisses felt different too. They still played like two happy puppies. But when they were tingling and needy and he rolled her to her back and entered her, their gazes caught and held. Everything she'd been thinking at the ball came into focus. He'd brought her into his world, and she'd belonged there.

Because she belonged with him and he belonged with her.

She made him laugh.

He cooked for her.

She loved touching him.

He stole her breath every time he looked at her—

They were now officially in too deep. Much deeper than they'd intended to go.

And as soon as he saw that, he would be gone.

Sunday, after breakfast and a try at the *Times* crossword puzzle, she walked into the bedroom and came out dressed in jeans and a sweater.

"If you don't mind, I need to finish my shopping."

Tossing the paper to a sofa cushion, he rose. "I don't mind. I'll come with you."

She pulled gloves out of her purse. "That's okay. You don't have to."

He headed for the bedroom to get his coat and shoes. "I want to."

He wanted to see what she looked at in stores. Because he wanted to buy her a Christmas gift.

It made him feel equal parts of happy and confused. He'd spent the past five years delegating his Christmas gift buying to his personal shopper, but he suddenly wanted to choose Autumn's present himself, even though he had no idea what she might want or need.

But her search for the perfect sweater for her dad and housecoat for her mom did not help him in the slightest. Neither did the thirty minutes she spent listening to a toy store owner discuss the merits of one train set over another.

"It's for my nephews," she'd told Jack as they walked out of the store with a starter set and onto the busy street again. "I promised my brother I'd get the train that they'll put under their tree. It had to be perfect. Something they can easily add to every year."

He snorted. "I know the importance of the right train. It took me and my mom an entire fall to find the one we eventually bought for under our Christmas tree—"

He stopped himself. The memory didn't hurt, but it did surprise him that he and Autumn had a shared experience. She wanted the right train for her nephews. He understood why.

They'd lived such different lives that it threw him for a second. But he shook his head to bring himself back to the present. Before his mom started Step Inside, he'd been raised in a blue-collar environment. Just as Autumn had been—

Maybe their lives weren't so different after all?

He froze, but quickly started walking again. The conversation had thrown him back in time for a few seconds, back to roots he'd all but forgotten he had because his life had changed so much, but also because he'd been very busy.

It was not a big deal.

Monday, he didn't even tell Autumn he'd be picking her up at six. Arnie simply pulled the limo in front of her building and she raced out, using her worn briefcase like an umbrella because today's snowflakes were huge and wet.

She jumped into the limo saying, "You were right! Gerry called me in today. We did my interview."

"And?"

She set her briefcase on the floor a few feet away from her boots. "And Friday at two I have a second interview with the board."

"The twenty-seventh?"

"Yeah."

"I thought they said they wanted somebody in place by the first of the year?"

"Looks like they're cutting it close."

"Technically they have until Tuesday."

She laughed. "I guess. But we get out at noon on

New Year's Eve—in case anybody has big plans, the charity gives us time to take a nap and get dressed. If they want someone in place when we return to work on January second, that means they have to announce their decision that morning."

He hugged her. "Doesn't matter. You got the second interview! That's great!"

She pondered that a second then said, "It is."

He frowned. "You seem to have lost your enthusiasm."

"There are four people interviewing with the board."

Arnie pulled the limo into traffic, heading for home.

He squeezed her hand. "You'll ace it."

"I think so. But it's difficult for me to get over the fact that I have to jump through hoops for this job."

He shrugged. "That's part of life."

She just looked at him.

"I'm serious. Things happen. And dreams don't fall from the sky. You have to work for them."

"I've been working for this for over five years."

"Look at this as your final push."

"Okay." She grinned at him. "So, what's for dinner?"

"What do you want?"

"First of all, I need to make sure you don't mind cooking."

The fact that she would even ask that shocked him. "I love to cook! I actually miss cooking."

"How good are you with soup?"

"I am *the man* when it comes to soup!"

"Turkey noodle?"

He winced. "Now, see… I have a problem coming up with that on the spur of the moment. I like to start with a carcass. You know, make my own broth."

"Seriously?"

"Think of me like an artist when it comes to food. Just like Picasso didn't do paint-by-number… I'm not a fan of recipes. Unless I create them. I make my own broth. Make my own sauces."

"What can you come up with for a spur of the moment dinner tonight?"

"Steak. Spaghetti—"

Her face brightened. "Oh, let's have spaghetti!"

"Okay. But tomorrow I'm getting a turkey. I'll brine it and stuff it—"

"That could be Christmas dinner!"

"You're having Christmas dinner with your parents."

Her voice turned pouty. "My mom makes ham."

"And you like turkey?"

"I *love* turkey."

The way she said it made him laugh. "Maybe we could eat the turkey on Saturday. By then you'll be sick of ham. I can spoil you."

* * *

Autumn liked the sound of that. As long as he was happy, she was happy. And planning dinners was a far cry from the emotionally charged night they'd had after the ball. It almost seemed like a return to normal. The kind of relationship they could handle.

They changed out of work clothes and into casual clothes and she watched him make spaghetti. He pulled out a bag of frozen noodles that he'd prepared from scratch and a bag of frozen sauce.

The whole time he thawed and prepared things, he talked about creating the dishes for Step Inside.

"It was like having a couple thousand anonymous judges. People don't hesitate to criticize you on social media…or compliment. I loved the challenge of it."

She took a sip of wine. "You sound like me when I need to choose the perfect floral arrangements for a summer gala. I never minded the criticism I got on the samples. I use it to make the arrangements better."

He gave her a taste of sauce. "What do you think?"

"I think your abilities are wasted running the company."

He chuckled and turned away, but the truth of that settled into her brain. His food was amazing and he was clearly happy cooking—

"How did you go from being the creative soul of the company to being the guy who looks at numbers? That couldn't have been easy."

"It was an adjustment."

"I'll bet." But he didn't say anything else. He didn't say, *It was an adjustment but now I love it.* He'd simply acknowledged the adjustment. He also wasn't enthusiastic about his job. Not the way he enjoyed cooking for her.

But he didn't seem to see it.

Just as she'd suspected, the spaghetti was so good, she groaned. "I can't imagine being this talented," she said, pointing at the spaghetti with meat sauce.

He ladled more sauce on her spaghetti as if he thought she hadn't taken enough. "I studied here in New York. After that I was working as a sous chef when Mom decided to open her restaurants. At first, it was just the one, but she had a dream."

"Have you ever considered that you inspired her dream?"

His eyebrows knit together when he frowned. "What?"

"You clearly have talent. She must have seen that and decided to create the vehicle you could use to skyrocket to stardom."

He laughed. "You have such an interesting way of looking at things."

She studied his face, seeking signs that he saw

what was going on in his own life. None came. He was clueless. "Or maybe I see things that you missed?"

He shook his head and dug into his spaghetti, the conversation dying a natural death as they talked about myriad other things as they ate.

When they were done, he rose to clear their dishes. She motioned him back down. "I'll clean up."

"You're a guest."

After the way they'd made love on Saturday night, that hit her funny and she stopped halfway to picking up his plate. She'd felt the difference in their feelings, the connection, the commitment to each other. Maybe he hadn't. But she had. If she looked at it that way, she knew his calling her a guest was meant to be positive, complimentary.

And, really, she wasn't supposed to be looking at this any other way than casual. That's all he wanted. That's all *she* wanted—

Wasn't it?

She took a breath and reached for his dish again. The short amount of time they'd known each other made his way of categorizing the relationship the smarter one. No matter that their crossover into stronger feelings had happened naturally. It was not in their plan. She had to get herself in line with him or she'd say or do something she'd regret.

She stacked the dishes in the dishwasher and tidied the kitchen while he checked his streaming service for a movie. They stayed up later than usual because neither one of them had work the next day, Christmas Eve. Remembering that, she also realized he didn't have a tree or any sort of Christmas decorations.

It didn't seem right that she'd be waking up Christmas morning in a house that didn't even have a nod to the holiday.

She woke early on Christmas Eve. Leaving him sound asleep in his comfortable bed, she tiptoed into the bathroom. After showering and dressing, she went out into the marshmallow world of accumulating snow. Fat, fluffy flakes tumbled around her as they billowed to the ground, toppling on piles of snow scraped off the sidewalk to the fronts of coffee shops, restaurants and boutiques.

Two hours later, with a small artificial tree and two boxes of ornaments, she had to call a car to take her home. Jack wasn't anywhere around when she stepped off the elevator into the penthouse but that simply made her surprise even better.

Halfway through assembling the tree, her phone rang. She plucked it from the sofa, saw the call was from her mom and answered. "Hey, Ma."

"Hey, yourself."

She'd never heard that discouraged tone from her mom and knew something had happened. "What's up?"

"Oven broke. No one's working on Christmas Eve. I can't get it fixed. And it's too late to go out and buy a new stove. It wouldn't be here by tomorrow. Which by the way is Christmas…so no one is working then, either."

She pressed her lips together to keep from laughing. The problem might be bad, but it wasn't the end of the world. "I'm sorry. I know this ruins your plans for Christmas dinner."

"I wanted a big dinner, but we can make do. I'm thinking tomorrow's lunch could be cold cuts and a cake, if there's a shop that still has a cake this close to Christmas." She sighed. "I should have baked the pies yesterday."

"It's not a big deal, Mom. Cold cuts will be fine."

The elevator door opened, and Jack walked out. He carried two huge bags into the kitchen and put them into the refrigerator before he strolled over to the sofa and bent to kiss her cheek. She smiled up at him.

"The family's accustomed to my brown sugar pineapple ham."

"No one cares about the ham, Ma. Everybody just wants to be together. Besides, without having to spend your morning in the kitchen you'll have more time to play with your grandkids."

"I suppose."

Frowning, Jack sat on the sofa beside her.

"Maybe I could hunt around Manhattan for a cake?"

"Manhattan? Are you at work? It's Christmas Eve! Don't you take a day off?"

She winced, realizing she'd nearly spilled the beans about being at Jack's. "I meant Queens."

"Okay. With all the shopping I have to do to change dinner, I'd appreciate it if you could bring dessert tomorrow."

"Consider it done."

"Thanks. I'll see you tomorrow around noon."

Autumn disconnected the call and Jack pulled her to him for a long, lingering kiss.

"I take it that was your mom."

"Yeah. Poor thing. Her oven broke. She can't bake the family ham and mashed potatoes…or her world-famous pumpkin pies."

"World-famous?"

"Well, maybe not world-famous. But the whole family loves them. They're a tradition. Still, I think she'll be okay with having sandwiches and cake tomorrow." She shrugged. "Not the big dinner she likes to make, but the point is getting the family together. She knows that and she'll be fine."

He nodded, then inclined his head toward the half-assembled Christmas tree. "I was going to ask you where you were when I finally rolled out of bed, but I figured it out. You should have woken me."

She laughed and kissed him again. "I knew you needed the sleep."

He chuckled.

She rose from the sofa and began inserting fake evergreen limbs into the pole that made up the spine of the artificial tree. "I also thought your house could use some holiday spirit."

He picked up one of the branches and examined it. "I haven't had a tree in forever." He caught her gaze. "Not even a fake one."

She'd bet he hadn't had a tree since his mom's passing, but she decided not to mention that. "Where did *you* go?"

"I did some shopping too. Got a turkey."

"Oh, for turkey noodle soup!"

"Yep. Also got a ham. Thought I'd make that for myself tomorrow—"

Jack stopped midsentence. In the butcher shop, choosing a turkey, he'd seen the ham and the Christmas decorations around the display case and suddenly wanted it. But there was a much better purpose for that ham.

"I could make your family's Christmas dinner."

"What?"

"Your family could come here, and I could make Christmas dinner."

Her eyes widened in horror. "Fate stole my mother's chance to make a ham. She's not going to agree to having Christmas anywhere but at her house."

He realized that in his spontaneity he'd forgotten they'd be outing themselves to her parents. She'd be too familiar with his house. He'd be too comfortable having her there. But he wanted to do this—

"Okay. I'll bake the ham here and we'll take it to your parents' house tomorrow."

"That's very nice of you, but—"

"Hey, your mom invited me to dinner. I know I'm welcome."

"Of course, you are! I just don't want you to go out of your way."

"It's not out of my way. We can get up early. I'll bake the ham and make some side dishes." The happy feelings he'd had standing in the butcher shop returned full force. The joy of really celebrating the holiday rushed through him. "It will be fun."

She bit her lower lip. "I should call my mother and tell her you're going to do that."

"You don't want it to be a surprise?"

"I don't want my mom and dad to be eating deli

meat from their freezer until August." Happiness suddenly filled her eyes, as if the merit of his idea finally sunk in for her. "Thank you. You're right. This could be fun."

He laughed as she picked up her phone to call her mom, but warmth filled him, as the spirit of Christmas warmed him. He'd liked her parents. It felt good to be able to do something nice for them.

He hadn't felt this way since he was nine, anticipating gifts and a special dinner. Candy in a stocking. Cookies left on the doorstep by neighbors. Carolers going from floor to floor of their apartment building, singing.

Crystal clear memories swept through him. Instead of brushing them away, he smiled and began planning the menu for Christmas dinner.

CHAPTER FIFTEEN

THEY WOKE EARLY the next morning, as Jack had said they would. He prepared the ham for baking then began making side dishes, sliding each one into storage containers as he completed them, then putting those containers into a thermal carrier.

"You're certainly prepared."

He peeked up at her. "Because I have storage containers?"

"No. The thermal thing. I didn't even know those existed."

He leaned across the center island and kissed her. "Because I'm guessing you don't cook, let alone take things to your mom's."

"Hey, I bought the cake."

"You and I are going to be the hit of the day."

He carted things to his Mercedes in the basement of the building. She scurried after him with the cake box, setting it beside the thermal container in the trunk. He'd baked the ham in an electric roaster not merely for ease of transport but to heat it before lunch. He took that to the car, then returned to the penthouse to help her carry the train for her nephews while she held a shopping bag of presents for her parents.

When they were finally settled on the front seat, she thought he'd start the car. Instead, he sat there for a few seconds, then reached into the pocket of the leather jacket he wore over a sage green sweater.

He handed her a small gift, obviously a wrapped jeweler's box. "I bought this for you. Merry Christmas."

Her heart stuttered. "Oh, I'm sorry. I didn't think we were doing presents."

He laughed. "If you're saying you didn't get me anything, I'm sort of glad. We've only been in each other's lives a few weeks. Presents might have been premature at this point." He paused to suck in a breath. "But I just wanted to buy you something." He peeked at her. "Myself." He sniffed a laugh. "It sounds weird when I say it out loud."

It sounded wonderful to her. It sounded like a man who was getting real feelings for her. Maybe even a guy who hadn't had real feelings for so long he didn't recognize them.

But she did. As long as she didn't push, he'd eventually come to the right conclusions.

He nudged his chin in the direction of the box. "Open it."

Her fingers shook slightly as she ripped the red foil paper from the box then opened it to reveal a diamond solitaire necklace. She wasn't an expert, but she'd seen one and two-carat solitaires. This one was bigger.

Her gaze jumped to his. "Oh, my God."

"You like it?"

She took it out of the box. When she held it up, the diamond caught even the dim light of the basement garage and sparkled like the sun. "It's beautiful."

"I just kept thinking that you have such a pretty neck, and this would be perfect nestled right there."

He tapped the little dip at the base of her throat before motioning for her to give him the necklace.

She handled it over and pulled her hair off her neck before turning around so he could fasten it at her nape. When he released the chain, the diamond fell exactly where he wanted it.

She faced him again and he smiled approvingly, proudly. "Just as I thought. It's perfect. Merry Christmas."

She'd never seen him so happy. Tears filled her eyes. "Merry Christmas." Such an ordinary thing to say, and an ordinary thing to do on Christmas Day, but the moment softened her bones and found a home in her heart. He might not realize it, but he loved her.

He started the car, but she put her hand on his forearm to stop him from putting it in gear. Then she leaned in and kissed him. "Thank you."

He smiled. "You're welcome."

They arrived at her parents around eleven, an hour before the other guests were to arrive. He pulled the Mercedes into the driveway of a white two-story house with black shutters. Very modest and traditional.

Carrying the roaster first, he followed Autumn to the front door. She entered without knocking. "Ma! Pop! Jack and I are here with lunch."

Her mother scrambled down the stairs as her dad lifted himself out of a recliner in a living room made small by the enormous Christmas tree in the corner.

"I've got the ham," Jack announced trailing Autumn as she led him to the kitchen. "We can plug in the roaster and it will be perfect by the time guests arrive."

Autumn's mom pressed her hands to her face. "This is wonderful!"

Unbuttoning her coat, Autumn leaned in and kissed her mom. "It's fabulous to live with a chef."

Her mom's head tilted in question.

Realizing what she's said, Autumn quickly covered her mistake. "I meant have a chef in your social circle." She shook her head as Jack exited the front door again to get his thermal bag of side dishes.

She quickly faced her mom. If her mom said or did the wrong thing, Jack could react badly. He wasn't skittish. He was careful. And they hadn't known each other long enough for him to endure her mom's well-meaning but pushy comments. This perfect dinner could end their relationship or at least send them back to square one.

"You promised no matchmaking. That also means no making something out of nothing."

Her mom straightened indignantly. "Well, I'm sorry for wanting the best for my daughter."

"And I would like the chance to choose my own partner."

Her mom rolled her eyes. "You've been making up your own mind since you were four. I do not think I'll change you now."

Her mom sauntered away as if she wasn't going to let anything ruin her good mood, and Autumn breathed a sigh of relief. She'd killed two birds with one stone in that short exchange. Her mom had been warned about matchmaking and Jack had been out of earshot.

Things were going well.

As Jack took care of business with lunch, her dad ambled into the kitchen, opened the refrigerator and pulled out two beers. He handed one to Jack, then twisted the cap on the second for himself. Jack reheated side dishes and tended to the ham, and Autumn's dad chitchatted with him about the Knicks.

Aaron soon arrived with his wife Penny and two boys, Mark and Donnie, who bounded over to Autumn, hugging her around the thighs.

She laughed with them, then chased them from the living room, through the dining room, into the kitchen and the foyer and back into the living room again. They shrieked with laughter when she caught them and tickled them, then the whole process started again until Autumn was so tired she had to sit.

Pete and his wife arrived late. But once they were out of their coats and settled in the living room, the opening of gifts began. Autumn sat on the floor beside the recliner, while Mark and Donnie distributed gifts. At six and four, neither could read, so they brought the packages to Autumn who read the tags before the boys took them to the appropriate receiver.

With the gifts opened, they moved to the dining room, where they ate the ham, hot potato salad, peas and pancetta, herb and garlic linguine, and creamed kale and mushrooms.

Her mom said, "This is fantastic."

"I didn't want to overstep by making your

pineapple ham and thought this would be a good replacement dinner until next year when your cooking will be the star again. Autumn tells me no one makes a pineapple ham like yours."

Mary blushed. "Well, I don't know about that."

"Your ham is great, Ma," Autumn said.

Aaron said, "Best around," as Pete said, "Absolutely the best."

Autumn smiled across the table at Jack, who winked at her, and she suddenly realized how modest he was. He didn't need to steal the show. He'd helped out—saved Christmas dinner—without making it a big deal.

Four-year-old Donnie strolled over to him with the car he'd gotten as a gift from Pete and Sasha. "It doesn't work."

Jack shifted on his seat and took the car from Donnie. Turning it over, he said, "Ah. You know why? It needs a battery."

Shaggy-haired Donnie blinked up at him.

Jack said, "It's a power source," then realizing who he was talking to he said, "It's what makes the car run."

Autumn bit back a laugh as her heart about exploded in her chest. She adored her nephews and having Jack be so kind to Donnie filled her with pleasure—then something else that made her swallow hard.

She could see Jack as a daddy.

No. She could see Jack as the father of *her* children. In this house for holidays. Laughing with her mom, talking about the Knicks with her dad.

She *loved* him. Deeply. Profoundly. So much her heart swelled to its breaking point.

It wasn't what she wanted.

But more than that, he wasn't ready.

Mary scrambled from her seat. "We have some batteries in the junk drawer."

Autumn's dad waved her down. "I'll get them. You eat."

Autumn did a doubletake as her dad rose from his chair and headed for the kitchen. He returned in a minute and handed the batteries to Jack who nimbly installed them and gave the car to Donnie.

"Press that little button there."

Donnie grinned, pressed the button and giggled when the toy car's engine came to life.

"Put it on the floor," Pete encouraged.

Donnie stooped down, placed the car on the floor and gasped when it raced from the dining room into the kitchen, stopping only when it hit the center island.

Everyone laughed. Donnie ran into the kitchen. Jack set his napkin on his plate and followed the little boy to the car. Mark quickly joined them.

Jack showed the two little boys the clear path for the car to run and they took turns hitting the start button, setting it on the floor, letting it run to the back door, then scooping it up and repeating the process.

Autumn watched them through the twenty minutes they played, wondering if Jack realized how good he was with kids.

And that he wanted a family?

Oh, he'd never say it. And she'd never even hint to him that his longing and joy were evident on his face and he played with her nephews…but it was there. She could see it. He wanted a family and she didn't.

Instead of watching the football game, as Jack assumed they would, the family cleared the table then set it up again for a game of Yahtzee.

At Jack's puzzled expression, Pete caught his elbow and dragged him a few feet back.

"Ma doesn't like football. So we play an hour or two of Yahtzee before we settle in like slugs."

"Okay."

They took seats around the dining table again. This time, instead of being across from Autumn, he found himself seated beside her. He remembered her warning about her mother and matchmaking, but he didn't have the sense that her mom had pushed them together. All he saw was what he believed to be the normal activities of family.

He and his mom had never been alone on

Christmas. She had too many friends. But they'd never had the simplicity of connection that he found here with the Jones family.

Kindness and laughter interspersed with teasing that usually led to more laughter.

Not familiar with the game, he'd come in dead last. Autumn's mom won, even letting Donnie roll her dice most of the time. Jim drank more beer, clearly unconcerned with positioning his dice rolls for maximum score. But Pete and Aaron had something of a competition that led to Pete coming in second and Aaron third, but only by three points.

Everybody laughed and joked, but by the time they were in the living room the Yahtzee scores were forgotten.

Around seven that night, it struck him that he hadn't once thought about leaving. He liked it at Autumn's parents' house. It wasn't the Christmas he was accustomed to with his mom. It was Christmas the way he'd imagined it when his friends talked about their holidays. What he believed "real" Christmas should be like.

He knew he was quiet as he drove back to the penthouse and realized neither he nor Autumn questioned where she'd spend the night. He pulled the Mercedes into his parking space. Autumn carried her gifts from her parents, and he carried the roaster which was big enough to hold the empty storage containers and thermal carrier.

They stepped off the elevator into the penthouse, totally silent. He assumed she was exhausted, maybe too tired to talk. It had been a long two days. But he was quiet because it all felt too normal.

Too, too normal.

Technically, he'd known Autumn for five years. But he had really only been in her life a few weeks. He'd met her parents three times. He'd only met her brothers that day.

How could this feel normal?

And why was it he hadn't missed his mom?

Hadn't *thought* of her except in passing all day.

Hadn't even considered going to the mausoleum with flowers as he did some Christmases.

Guilt overwhelmed him. His mother had been the center of his world. She had also provided him with an opportunity to be the creative center of Step Inside. He didn't believe, as Autumn had said, that she'd opened a restaurant to give him a place to showcase his talent. But he did see that those years he'd spent planning menus and creating recipes for her company had been a gift of a sort.

And he'd forgotten her.

It rattled through him, made him feel odd, itchy like he couldn't reconcile it in his brain.

"I think I'll shower," he said as they stepped into the bedroom. He walked toward the bathroom, pulling his sweater over his head, not waiting for Autumn's reply.

In the bathroom, he turned on all the jets and grabbed his bodywash. The shower steamed enough that he didn't see Autumn enter until she opened the glass door and walked inside to join him.

Without a word, she slid against his soapy torso, put her arms around his neck and kissed him. He fell into the kiss like a drowning man, which only confused him more. When the diamond solitaire at her throat winked at him, something sensual and possessive raced through him and he kissed her hotly, greedily, as he ran the luffa down her back, then let it fall to the shower floor, replacing it with his hands.

Laughing, she slid away, but he caught her wrist and brought her back, so he could nuzzle the shiny spot at her throat and let his hands touch every inch he couldn't reach with his lips. Sliding both palms up her sides, he let them meet below her breasts, lifting them for his eager mouth. She moaned as he pulled on each one, then she wrapped one leg around his thighs.

Power coursed through him when he realized she'd positioned them perfectly. He angled himself to enter her, then shifted their positions so that he could sit on the shower bench with her straddling him. When they were settled, he let his lips roam from her shoulders to her stomach and back up again. She tensed, trembling and began the rhythm that brought them both to a fever pitch of need.

Her release came first, rippling around him, bringing him to the point of no return.

After that they showered for real, and he'd never felt more energized and yet more exhausted. The crazy push pull between guilt and happiness happening in his brain had been silenced while they were in the shower, but it seemed to be back again. Guilt wanted to drag him down. Even as happiness bubbled through him.

Telling himself to stop thinking, he toweled off Autumn's back and she returned the favor, which led to kissing again.

Wonderful kisses that reached the entire way to his soul and filled up empty places he always knew were there but couldn't reach himself. They kissed their way to the bedroom and fell into bed where they made love again and eventually drifted off into an exhausted sleep.

But in the last seconds of consciousness, it struck him that even the fleeting thoughts or memories he'd had of his mom had always evaporated into nothing that day.

It was like he couldn't hold on to them.

Like losing her again.

Which made him wonder how in the hell he could allow himself to be happy, when he was forgetting the person who hadn't merely raised him; she'd given him a wonderful life.

CHAPTER SIXTEEN

HE WOKE THE next morning to find Autumn gone. He rolled out of bed, slid into sweatpants and a sweatshirt and headed for the main area.

When he reached the living room, he saw her in the kitchen, toasting bagels.

She walked over and kissed him. "We had so much rich food to eat yesterday, I thought we should go back to basics…bagels."

Scrubbing his hand across the back of his neck, he laughed. He loved having her with him and wished he could figure out, and to make his peace with, his guilt and sorrow. Especially when Autumn herself was one of the reminders of his remorse. He'd been with her the night his mom had died.

In fact, being with her had taken away his opportunity to change the outcome of that night.

If he hadn't been with Autumn, he might have gotten his mom the medical help she needed—

"I also wanted to thank you for being so good to my parents yesterday. My whole family really."

He fought the guilt, the memories of the night his mom died, and forced himself into the present. "Your family is very easy to get along with."

The toaster popped. She took out two sides of the first bagel and offered them to him. "You have cream cheese, right?"

"Of course, I have cream cheese."

She laughed, then kissed him again.

The world righted for a few seconds then quickly fell off-kilter again because he could not understand how all this could feel so perfect, so right, when inside he was angry with himself. He stood in the center of his fancy kitchen, holding two halves of a bagel, looking like a tourist in Times Square, not sure which way to turn.

She opened the refrigerator, retrieved the cream cheese and set it on the center island.

He shook his head, hoping to clear these feelings, as he prepared his bagel.

"Of course, we could eat them plain to give our stomachs the chance to balance out."

He said nothing, simply took his bagel to the side of the center island that offered seating, set it on a napkin and then walked to the coffeemaker. Silence hung in the air as she put cream cheese on her bagel and his coffee brewed.

When both were finally seated at the island the silence wasn't merely obvious, it was telling.

He knew he couldn't get himself out of his own

head. Couldn't fight the guilt over having had such a good day.

He had no idea why Autumn was quiet.

She took a breath. "Okay, look. I know yesterday had to be hard for you."

"You just said you appreciated how good I was with your family. Now, you're saying you could tell the day was difficult for me?"

"You didn't get quiet until we were in the car. Then you were odd when we got home."

"You didn't seem to think so in the shower."

She laughed and caught his gaze. "You were your normal self then."

He couldn't reply. Not because she was wrong. Because he hated that she wanted to talk about this when he wasn't even sure what to say.

"I think it's perfectly normal for someone to decompress after meeting so many new people, but there's more. You really seemed to enjoy cooking dinner for my parents."

"I did."

"And they loved it and you loved that they loved it."

"What's wrong with that?"

"Nothing. That's my point. You've been cooking and talking about cooking so much that it struck me last night that I think you might be missing how cooking is becoming part of your life again."

That was far, far away from what he'd been thinking last night, but for some reason or another it resonated. Which was stupid considering all the misery and guilt he'd been experiencing. "You think I miss cooking?"

"Yes."

Suddenly, the truth of that rippled through him. Experiencing grief and guilt had tried to drown it out, but she was right. He'd enjoyed making Christmas dinner. He'd enjoyed cooking in a way he hadn't in years—

He blocked the thought, but it wouldn't go away because these feelings weren't new. He'd been having them since he'd begun cooking for Autumn. He'd gotten so good at blocking them he didn't even feel them pop up anymore.

That thought spiraled into more thoughts. He could see himself cooking for her forever. But he could also see that though that might be fulfilling for a while, it was not a permanent solution—

Solution?

To the guilt? That didn't make sense.

"You know, you haven't spoken a lot about your mother, but you've said enough that I've guessed some things."

He glanced over at her.

"You've told me that you're keeping her dream alive. Maybe building her dream."

He cautiously said, "I am."

"And you believe her dream was to have a bunch of really great restaurants."

"A business. Not necessarily restaurants. My mom wanted to run a business. She was incredibly smart. She took night classes at community college, thought things through and ultimately wanted to create a successful business."

Her face softened as she put her hand on his forearm, as if comforting him. "When did the desire to start a chain of restaurants come up for her?"

"After I did some apprenticeships, we both saw that I had some unique abilities and she realized that was her chance."

"What if that wasn't what happened?"

He peered at her.

"What if she saw your potential as a chef and she started her business as a way to give *you* a platform?"

She'd mentioned something like that before, but it didn't fit. "My mom had always wanted to start a business. Because she'd been a waitress and hostess and even a general manager of a diner, restaurants seemed like a good fit."

"Jack, I know I may be overstepping here. But watching you cook for me all week and how you enjoyed it… I felt like I understood what your mom felt watching you. She might have always wanted to start a business, but she didn't even try until you showed promise."

He stared at her.

"I think what she really wanted was for you to continue research and development. To make Step Inside extraordinary because of your talent."

His temper hummed below his skin. "Are you saying Step Inside wasn't her dream?"

"It was very much her dream. Her dream *for you*. I think that when you lost her, you got it backwards. I think she wanted you in R&D. Not taking the place she had."

The hum became red hot anger. "Stop. Just stop. That wasn't how it was."

She held up her hands. "I'm not saying this to make you mad. I'm not saying that you have to change. I'm just giving you something to think about, something to consider."

"Because I've been moody?"

"Sort of. But more because you're wasting your talents."

"Well, thank you very much." He rose from the stool, his anger so hot and so potent he could have easily said something he would regret. Heading for the bedroom, he said, "I'm going in to work today. I'll text Arnie's number to you and you can have him drive you home." He turned and faced her. "Unless you'd rather take the subway. Isn't that what you do? Resist everybody's help or opinion. Even though you don't hesitate to share your own."

"That's not fair! Especially since you all but coached me for the CEO position."

He said, "Hmmm." And headed for the bedroom again. She was right. She had taken his help and now she was offering hers and it infuriated him. Not because he didn't like assistance or opinions but because she was wrong! She thought she had his whole life figured out when he didn't even have his life figured out!

He dressed quickly and was returning to the main area before she'd finished her bagel.

Without a word, he walked past her, shrugging into his leather jacket. Knowing no one else would be in the office, he'd worn jeans and a sweater, so the jacket worked.

And his Mercedes keys were in the pocket.

Autumn watched him go. A million questions swam in her head. She could think their disagreement small, meaningless, a blip, something they would laugh about that evening when he returned.

Except—with his offer of a ride from Arnie— he'd kicked her out.

She bit her lower lip, thinking this through. Technically, they'd been living together. Without getting to know each other they'd fallen into a serious living arrangement and with their first fight hanging in the air, she realized she needed time as much as he needed time.

Whether he saw it or not, he was changing. His life was changing. What he wanted was changing.

And she might be getting her big break. A break that didn't mesh with the new things he wanted.

She didn't call Arnie. Instead, she gathered her things with an eye toward carrying them on the subway. She left behind the dresses and items he'd bought her. Not just because they wouldn't fit into the duffel bag she'd used, but because they weren't hers.

When all the clothes and cosmetics she'd brought were stuffed in the duffel, she touched the solitaire at her throat.

He'd given that to the woman he had fun with. Not the one who'd tried to get him to see that he might have taken his life down the wrong path.

She reached behind her to undo the clasp, slid it off and set it on the table in his walk-in closet. He liked fun Autumn. He didn't seem to like more serious Autumn or maybe he didn't like *anyone* questioning his life choices.

She couldn't say. They hadn't been together long enough for her to know that.

Rolling her duffel behind her, she headed for the main room and the elevator. They definitely needed some time apart. If he called her and they smoothed things over, the solitaire would be on the table in the closet.

If he didn't—
She refused to think about that.

Jack returned home from work, half expecting Autumn to be there. As he rode the private elevator, nerves skittered through him. He didn't want to have a fight, but he didn't want her in the penthouse. No one had the right to question his decisions about Step Inside. Someone who didn't know his mother had even less right to an opinion.

Plus, that morning at work, his world had seemed to right again. All those crazy feelings he'd had at breakfast had disappeared.

So what if his penthouse seemed cold and empty without Autumn? So what if he missed cooking for her, missed the eager expression on her face before she took her first bite of whatever he'd made her? Something about being alone felt right.

Friday morning his staff returned to work and even more order came to his world. Contracts arrived, resumes for new chefs were stacked on his desk, blueprints for the new restaurants to be built in Pennsylvania were delivered.

He dove in eagerly, but by eleven he'd looked at the details on the drawings so long his eyes crossed. Telling himself that was normal, he called the architects, and they came to his office to meet with him. As they spoke, it struck him that they were competent enough that he shouldn't be making decisions that they were more quali-fied to make.

Worse, after the architects were gone, he tried to read the five-year plan, but it bored him so much, he stuffed it in his briefcase to read over the weekend while watching a game.

An itchy feeling trembled along his nerve end-ings. He refused to try to identify it.

Autumn had had her interview with the board of directors for Raise Your Voice Friday after-noon, and as Jack had said, she aced it. She should have been happy. Instead, she kept getting weird thoughts about whether or not a CEO had enough time to raise children.

The very thought shocked her. Never in her life had she thought she'd want to have kids. She loved her nephews, but they hadn't made her long to have her own child until she'd seen Jack with those rambunctious little boys.

Thinking about Jack made her catch her breath. He'd arranged for her to leave Thursday and all of Friday had gone by without a word.

She'd noticed that they were both changing. He wanted more out of life than to run his mom's company. He wanted a family and suddenly she wanted kids. Not to accommodate him but because it seemed right.

But he wouldn't talk about it. He hated when she mentioned his returning to research and development. What would he think if she brought up kids?

He'd probably explode as he had the morning after Christmas.

Had she pushed him? Had she believed she'd seen something that wasn't there?

She knew she hadn't. She knew what she'd seen. She'd been trying to help, but he didn't want help. So now she knew his boundaries. She wouldn't breach them again. She'd forget about having kids. Forget about Step Inside. Not second guess anything about his life.

Because he would call. He was a smart guy. They had a casual relationship. Eventually, his anger would cool, and he'd remember how much fun they'd had.

But when he didn't call Friday night, she knew this wasn't a blip in their relationship. Like five years ago, he'd simply walked away from her. Every time she glanced at her silent phone, every time she peered out the window, hoping to see his Mercedes pull in her driveway, she felt the awful ache of reality.

He'd left her once and never looked back.

He had done it again. He might have asked her

to leave his apartment, but he'd done the asking and now he was ghosting her.

Saturday morning, she woke knowing she had to get her thoughts off Jack. Her comments at breakfast the day after Christmas hadn't been an accusation but were meant to be the start of a discussion. But that wasn't how he'd taken them, and she couldn't turn back the hands of time.

She forced her thoughts to her interview with the Raise Your Voice board. Not one person on the board had a problem with her until Quincy Fallen had asked about her relationship with Ivy. She'd kept her response brief, then shifted the conversation to her knowledge and experience with Raise Your Voice and most of the members had nodded with approval—

But what if Quincy was a holdout? Could one negative vote ruin her chances of being appointed CEO?

And what would it be like not to be able to tell Jack? To commiserate. To have him remind her there would be other opportunities?

She groaned. She'd circled back to Jack! Why did she want a guy who had no problem leaving her?

And why did it hurt so much that he'd simply told her to leave his apartment? No discussion. No chance for her to think it through and apologize—

Because that's how their last foray into a relationship had ended. With him simply deciding it was over. And never calling her again.

Angry with herself, she grabbed her jacket and mittens, as well as clothes for an overnight stay and called a ride share to take her to her parents' house.

When she finally arrived after lunch, she hoisted her duffel over her shoulder and headed for the front door. It opened before she could reach it and her mom frowned at her.

"What are you doing here?" She eyed the duffel. "Are you planning on doing laundry?"

"No. I thought I could watch a little basketball with Pop and maybe we could play a game tonight."

"Your dad's at Tony's with his friends. But he'll be back in a few hours." Her mother took the duffel from her shoulder and guided her inside the foyer. "So if this isn't laundry, you must have brought clothes to stay overnight?"

She shrugged.

"You're not going out with Jack tonight?"

She peeked over at her mom. "No." She struggled with tears. She was tired. She was hurt. But more than that, she couldn't escape the feeling that she'd overstepped her boundaries and hurt *him*.

And that was what was really bothering her.

She'd missed something. They'd had other discussions of his mother's death and vague discussions about his taking over Step Inside. Not enough for her to know his entire story, but enough that she should have known not to speak until she could do so intelligently.

But she'd pushed ahead.

Because she'd been so sure she was correct about Step Inside.

It hurt that she'd lost him. But she ached over the realization that she could have hurt him.

Avoiding her mom's eyes, she said, "Let's go make cookies or something."

Shaking her head, her mom walked to the kitchen. "Okay. Don't tell me. I'm happy to distract you with cookie making. You're also lucky that the oven is fixed. Your nephews will be here tomorrow afternoon. They like snickerdoodles and chocolate chip. We'll make both."

Relief rippled through her until watching her mom mix batter reminded her of watching Jack cook. She grabbed the recipe and began locating ingredients for her mom to add. That made her feel marginally better.

But when her dad came home, the cookies were cooling and the game was at halftime, the achy, horrible realization that she was alone rolled over her again. Not because she didn't have someone but because *she* hurt Jack.

She was going to have to go to his penthouse and apologize.

Of course, that didn't mean he'd take her back.

But at least she'd have the chance to admit she'd been wrong.

She sucked it up, retrieved her duffel from her old bedroom, called a car and said goodbye to her parents.

She didn't like the idea of carrying her duffel bag into his penthouse, then realized if things went well, it would be good to have clothes for tomorrow morning.

With a deep breath to encourage herself, she walked into the lobby.

Josh, the doorman, stopped her. "Miss Jones."

She smiled. "Yes… Oh, wait! I probably don't have today's elevator code."

He chuckled. "You're also out of dress code."

"Excuse me?"

"It's a party, remember?"

It took a second for that to sink in. When it did, she swore her heart exploded. While she'd been upset for days, worried that she'd overstepped her boundaries and hurt his feelings, he'd been planning a party?

She forced herself to smile at Josh. "You know what? I forgot." She took two steps backward, toward the lobby door. "And I'm not going up in jeans."

Josh laughed. "There's some pretty fancy dresses in that penthouse right now."

She smiled again, but she had to grit her teeth to keep it in place. "I'll bet."

She turned and raced out into the frigid night. The cloudless sky was inky black. The marshmallow snow had become dirty gray from days of pedestrians walking on it. She picked up her pace and told herself to call a ride share but the humiliation cut too deep.

When would she learn that Jack Adams wasn't ever going to love her?

And why did a realization that should have been common sense hurt so much?

Jack woke the next morning to silence so thick and so total it reminded him of the day after his mother's funeral. He'd lived alone, but he'd stayed in his mother's penthouse that night, simply to make things easier.

But he'd woken to the reality that he was alone. Truly alone. He'd woken to the realization that his selfish desire to spend the night with Autumn might have caused her death. Her cardiologist had told him that her condition had been severe and that his getting her to the hospital sooner *might* have saved her...but his professional opinion was that a few extra minutes probably wouldn't have made a difference.

So he'd woken in her penthouse, knowing she was gone, knowing he was in charge and so tired he wasn't sure he could think.

Today, he didn't have that problem. The party the night before had been filled with executives who were happy to give him their opinions. He had a million possibilities floating around in his head about how to expand Step Inside, and no desire to work toward fulfilling any one of them.

He rolled out of bed, strolling to the kitchen in a navy-blue silk robe that cost more than his mother had made in a year when she was raising him on a waitress's salary.

He made a cup of coffee, and read the *Times*, which had been brought to his penthouse by whoever was manning the lobby desk. He didn't think about Autumn; just as he had after his mom died, he'd blocked her from his thoughts.

But his heart hurt, and his head about exploded from the waterfall of good ideas that had been presented to him the night before…and behind all that was guilt.

Not that his mom had died but that he was living her dream and he didn't appreciate it.

He ran his hands down his face, showered and dressed in jeans, a leather jacket and sunglasses. Without clouds, the sun was a ruthless ball in the sky that didn't provide warmth this frigid Sunday. It only glared down at him.

Arnie awaited at the curb. Holding the back door of the limo, he said, "Good morning, sir."

"No *sir*," Jack growled. "Just Jack…remember?"

"Yes, sir… I mean, Jack."

Jack slid inside. Arnie closed the door. When he was behind the steering wheel, he said, "Where to?"

"New Jersey… The mausoleum."

Arnie caught his gaze in the rearview mirror. He'd been Jack's driver for years. He knew exactly what Jack was talking about. "Okay."

Jack stared out the window as they drove to his mother's resting place. Almost an hour later, they pulled onto the winding road. Trees typically thick with green leaves stood bare and empty.

When they reached the building, Arnie stopped. Jack got out without a word.

He walked into the silent space. Beautifully appointed with murals in the domed ceiling and gold trim, the echoing room spoke of peace and tranquility.

He ambled to the bench closest to his mom's space and sat.

"I haven't been here in a while." The quiet of the room greeted him. No reply. Not even his own imaginings of what his mother might say.

He sat in the silence. Sorrow for her loss and faded memories filled the air. But he couldn't hold them. They all withered away.

Into nothing.

Alone in the cold bleak room, he wondered what he was doing there. There were no answers in the mural. There were no answers in the silence of the room.

He lifted himself from the bench, walked over and touched the gold-plated square that held his mom's name.

He longed for her to be in his life, but he didn't cry. She'd been gone five years. He missed her laugh. He missed her crazy sense of humor. He missed her smart-as-a-whip way of running Step Inside.

But she wasn't here and nothing about the past could be changed—

And life had gone on.

Arnie drove him home and Jack handed him the tickets for the next Knicks game to thank him for working on a Sunday.

Arnie beamed. "Jack! Thank you. You don't have to do this…" He laughed. "You do pay me."

Jack shook his head and walked toward the lobby doors. "Take your son."

As the word *son* spilled out of his mouth, his chest tightened. He always thought of himself as a *son*. But the way the word rippled through him was different this time.

He waved at the doorman as he ambled to the elevator, then rode it up to the penthouse.

The place was as sterile and empty as he re-membered. He walked through to the bedroom, into the closet where he hung his jacket, took off his sweater and exchanged it for a T-shirt.

Turning to go, he saw a wink of light and stopped. Sitting on the counter of the closet table was the necklace he'd given to Autumn.

If he closed his eyes, he could feel the soft skin his fingers had grazed as they fastened it around her neck. He could see the look of surprise on her face. He could her the whisper in her voice when she thanked him. He could feel her kiss.

His heart stumbled.

He lowered himself to the bench beside the table.

His mother was gone.

The life she wanted was over.

He'd fulfilled her dream.

But *his* dream had frozen in time.

And Autumn had seen that.

He hadn't gotten mad at her because what she'd suggested was absurd. He'd gotten angry because it wasn't. The time had come for him to move on and he didn't want to see it.

He should have seen it. Having Autumn walk into his life again, bring him joy, should have been a clear sign. The way she'd filled the empty spaces in his soul felt like he'd been waiting for her.

But he was too busy trying to have the futur

and the past—too busy working at something that was wrong for him—to see he'd been waiting for Autumn to somehow come back into his life. She hadn't been Cinderella waiting for the Prince to find her again. He'd been the Prince, working through his grief, straightening out his life. So that when she came back into his life, he'd been ready for her.

The love of his life.

The love of his life...

Oh, God. She was the love of his life. The rest of his life. But having dumped her again, he'd blown their second chance.

She'd be crazy to even answer a phone call from him, let alone love him.

CHAPTER SEVENTEEN

AUTUMN HAD SPENT the Saturday night and most of Sunday crying. She couldn't believe it was possible to fall in love in four weeks, but she had. And losing Jack this time was worse than waking up to find him gone after a one-night stand.

After four weeks together she knew he was wonderful, kind, smart and imaginative. They were meant to be together.

But how could they ever be together? How could Fate possibly believe they were meant to be together when they kept screwing things up?

First, he ghosted her.

Now she'd hurt him.

And he wouldn't talk about it. Everything wrapped up in his past seemed to be off limits.

They were doomed. And she decided it was time she accept that.

Jack Adams might not want her, but someone would.

She was a catch.

She might not have seen that before he'd

waltzed back into her life, but she did now. Not just because she had a shot at becoming a CEO—and even if she didn't get it, there were other charities in New York City that could use her expertise—but because she finally realized she wanted a family.

She strode into work on Monday morning so confident she could have fought a tiger. She hung her coat on a hook and tossed her purse into her old metal desk, knowing that if Raise Your Voice didn't want her, she was ready to job hunt.

She would forget about Jack—eventually. She simply had to plow through a few weeks of a broken heart, knowing she'd caused it herself.

But Monday went by without Gerry making an announcement about the new CEO. Still, she calmed herself with the reminder that they had one more day, December thirty-first, to make their decision.

Tuesday, she dressed for work in a somber mood. If they didn't offer her the job that day, she'd be reading the name of the new Raise Your Voice CEO in Thursday's *Times*.

So she walked into the office with her head high, reminding herself there were other charities who needed CEOs. She might not get the job as the CEO for Raise Your Voice, but she would begin her quest for a CEO position somewhere. And she would someday be running a charity.

"Can I see you for a minute?"

Autumn glanced up to see Gerry standing in her doorway. She rose from her seat. "Sure."

He led her down the hall to his office and closed the door behind her. Her heart stopped. He was so somber he could be about to tell her that she didn't get the job.

Motioning for her to take a seat, he walked to his desk chair. "As you've probably guessed, we've made a decision about the CEO position."

Her breath stuttered. This was it. She got the job, or she moved on. It almost didn't matter either way. She'd lost Jack but she planned on getting back out into the dating pool and looking for someone who would really love her. She could lose this position. She would apply for other jobs.

She had found herself as a woman and a worker. She would not lose that.

Gerry said, "Congratulations! You've got the job."

Her mouth fell open. Here she was, ready to start making copies of her new resume, expecting the worst. Getting good news shocked her.

"I'm..."

"Speechless." Gerry laughed. "We would like to announce on January second, so that gives you about twenty-four hours before we need your answer."

She burst out laughing, even as her heart tweaked

with longing to call Jack and tell him she'd gotten the job. Maybe to thank him for his help. Probably because she still loved him. He was a great guy. And she wasn't entirely sure how she'd gotten everything wrong, but she had and she had no one to blame but herself for losing him.

Knowing that didn't help. It only made her heart ache. But she pulled herself together and forced herself into the moment.

She might have lost the man she loved, but she'd gained the job she'd been working for forever. She had to get her head back in the game.

Gerry handed a folder across the desk. "This is the full benefit package and the formal written offer." He rose. "I hope you'll accept."

She stood. "You know what? I don't need twenty-four or thirty-six hours. I've wanted this job forever." She reached across the desk to shake his hand. "I'm your new CEO."

"Congratulations!"

She took a breath. "Thanks." But despite her bravado, her chest hollowed out. She was getting what she'd worked for since the day she walked into the Raise Your Voice offices. But she wasn't getting what she wanted.

The only reason she wanted to be a mom was because she wanted Jack's kids. She wanted to raise kids with Jack. To instill in them his sense of humor and drive. And hope they got a thing or two from her too.

Getting the job didn't exactly feel meaningless, but she now knew there was more to life than work, and she wasn't sure what to do about that.

She turned to go but Gerry stopped her. "Oh, I almost forgot." He reached into a desk drawer and handed her two tickets.

"Those are tickets for Audrey Brewbaker's annual New Year's Eve party tonight. I'm not CEO anymore." He smiled. "You are. Because we're not announcing until January second, you can't actually talk Raise Your Voice business. But you can go, look around, figure out who you need to schmooze. You never know when you'll have to replace a board member or need a benefactor to fund a special project."

He laughed and she smiled, looking at the tickets as if they were foreign things. But she'd longed for this challenge, and she was up to it. She simply might need the whole day not just the afternoon to get ready for her first party as newly appointed CEO.

She walked out of Gerry's office, directly into hers, grabbed her purse and coat and headed home, refusing to let herself think about the fact that she'd gotten what she'd always wanted but she wasn't complete. There was a hole in her heart.

Still, she would fix it. Without Jack. He'd rejected her twice. She got the message.

CHAPTER EIGHTEEN

JACK WALKED INTO the ballroom for Audrey Brewbaker's annual New Year's Eve party, not feeling very much like schmoozing or dancing or even eating dinner. But he'd RSVP'd for two, when he believed he would be taking Autumn. He couldn't back out completely. He would say hello to the hosts, eat dinner and then race home.

After greeting Audrey and her daughter Marlene in the reception line, he walked farther into the ballroom and saw a swatch of red. The same color as the gown Autumn had worn to the Montgomerys' Christmas party.

She was here?

Telling himself he was crazy, he edged over to the bar, but he saw the red again and *knew* it was the same gown.

His heart did a flip. But as the bartender poured him a bourbon, he reminded himself that her being here was a long shot. She needed a ticket to get in.

Still, when he turned from the bartender, his

bourbon in hand, he couldn't stop himself from scouting for the red again. He found it and saw her, and his stomach fell to the floor, but his brain clicked in. If he genuinely believed Fate had brought her back into his life because he'd been waiting for her and was finally ready, then he had to have the guts to face her.

He worked his way through the crowd that milled around the linen-covered tables and after ten minutes of following her from one group of people to the next, he finally caught up to her.

"Hey."

Obviously recognizing his voice, she turned. "Hey."

"I'd really like five minutes to talk to you."

She smiled…that same smile that she'd given him at Ivy and Sebastian's the night they'd all had dinner together. The fake one.

"That would be fun," she said, not meaning a word of it. "But I'm not really here as a guest." She winced. "Well, I am a guest. But I'm also CEO of Raise Your Voice."

She'd gotten the job! "That's great!"

"Yes. And I know I owe it to you. But I'm also here to make connections." She stepped to the right. "If you'll excuse me."

And just like that, she was gone.

He started after her, but she really was talking with people Jack knew were benefactors for charities. Good business sense kept him from interrupting her or joining her groups, making her nervous on what was—technically—the first day of her new job.

Dinner was served and he tried to find Autumn but couldn't. Audrey Brewbaker's New Year's Eve party was the party of the year in Manhattan. There had to be four hundred people in attendance and lots of women wore red gowns.

After Audrey's thank-you-for-attending comments and wishes for everyone to have a wonderful New Year, the band began to play.

As people ambled onto the dance floor, the crowd thinned, and Jack spotted Autumn. He was not leaving without apologizing or better yet, explaining.

He'd run out on her the first time. Though he had a good excuse, he would not run out on her a second time. He would explain. He would apologize.

He eased through the tables toward hers. Four steps before he reached her, she rose and headed to the right.

Close enough to reach her, he caught her wrist and stopped her. She turned and looked at him.

Everything inside him melted with need. He could see their future. But he didn't deserve it and even if he did he had no idea how to tell her that. He released her wrist but couldn't resist the urge for one final dance.

"Dance with me."

"I don't know—"

"Please. I need to apologize."

The surprised expression on her face confused him. She glanced left then right, then caught his gaze. "I thought I needed to apologize. I was hoping, though, to see you in a more private place."

"No one even cares we're here." He waited a second then said, "Dance with me."

This time when she smiled at him, he saw the real Autumn. He held out his hand and she took it. They reached the dance floor as one song ended, and another began.

"A waltz."

She shook her head. "Looks like the heavens are smiling down on you."

He laughed. "Yeah. I literally get to put my best foot forward."

He took her into his arms and glided them out onto the dance floor. Autumn's heart lurched. Nothing had ever felt so right as dancing with him. She'd never had the feelings for another man that she had for him. To be this close physically and so far away emotionally was a pleasure-pain too intense to describe.

"I just..." He paused. "I need to tell you that I'm sorry. What I was going through on Christmas Day was nothing like either one of us thought. I thought I was feeling guilty that I had forgotten my mom. But the truth is I think Fate was trying to tell me it was time to move on."

She pulled back so she could see his eyes. She hated that he had gone through that. Hated even more that she'd made it worse. "And I'm sorry I said those things about your mom's real plan."

"No. You might have been right." He swung them around the dance floor in a flawless waltz. "It's been five years. I did everything my mom had planned, but I'd gotten bored with it. Cooking for you nudged me to remember how much I loved it."

Surprised, she said only, "Oh."

"And that's not all I want to say to you... What made me realize I needed to move on was how much I missed you."

Their gazes caught and clung. "I missed you too."

"The night we met, I knew I'd found the person I wanted to spend the rest of my life with."

Her heart stuttered.

"Then everything went wrong, and I almost forgot you."

"I thought you had forgotten me."

"I sort of had until I saw you at Ivy and Sebastian's. You came out the door when I was waiting by Sebastian's limo and I couldn't believe it."

Not sure what to say, she only held his gaze.

"I'd hardly thought of you in five years and

suddenly there you were. I realized today that Fate hadn't brought you back into my life until I was ready for you…ready to move on. And in the five years we were apart, I chose the three worst women to have a relationship with because I think deep down I knew I was waiting for you."

She blinked up at him. "I'm not sure if that's the craziest thing I've ever heard or the most romantic."

"Make it the most romantic thing you've ever heard because I really believe we're a match. I've never felt about anyone what I feel about you. I don't want to."

Her heart swelled at the romance of it, but she had to be sure they were on the same page. "Now it's my turn. I realized on Christmas Day that I didn't just want to be the CEO for Raise Your Voice. I want to have kids. *Your* kids. I want the whole thing. I don't want to be the second half of the power couple you envisioned. I want more. I want it all. I want the fairytale."

He whirled her around. "Really?"

"Think that through because you will not get a chance to leave me a third time. There will be no charm in your life if you ghost me again."

"How many kids are you thinking?"

The interest in his voice gave her enough courage to say, "How many kids are you thinking…"

He considered that. "One of each I guess."

"Seriously? You saw how much fun Mark and Donnie have. You need two of each so they can be friends."

He laughed. "We do have enough money that we could hire help."

"A nanny? My mother would shoot me if we shut her out."

"Looks like we're going to need a bigger penthouse."

"Or a house in Hunter."

He frowned. "Near your parents?"

"Why not?"

He looked at her for a few seconds, then smiled. "Why not?"

The music stopped but instead of pulling away, they stepped closer and kissed.

Dancers walked by them, couples exiting or entering the floor.

They kept kissing.

When the music began again, he pulled away and they headed for the coatroom. She texted Arnie as he found their coats.

A half hour later, they were kissing their way to the bedroom. When they reached it, he stopped. "Hold on a second."

She frowned. "What?"

He held up one finger. "Just give me a second."

She shook her head, but he returned quickly. "Turn around."

Confused, she only stared at him.

He held up her necklace. "You must have forgotten this the day after Christmas."

She smirked. "Must have."

He laughed, fastened the necklace around her neck and gave her a little nudge that tumbled her to the bed.

"I love you."

She froze. Her eyes filled with tears. "I don't think we've ever said that."

"Well, now that we have, let's not stop."

She smiled. "I love you, too."

EPILOGUE

THEY WERE MARRIED on Valentine's Day two years later. Believing Ivy and Sebastian had brought them back together, they asked Ivy to be maid of honor and Sebastian to be best man.

They held the wedding in the same venue Sebastian and Ivy had, Parker and Parker. The castle-like building stood tall in the thick February snow, as Autumn raced inside, Ivy holding her long lace train. Her entire dress was lace and her headpiece a tiara that sparkled in her reddish-brown hair.

In the bride's room, her mother fussed, but her dad grinned. He loved the new addition to their family. Not just because Jack had Knicks season tickets but because he was a great guy. They waited in the quiet room with four full-length mirrors and ornate French Provincial furniture until the wedding planner opened the door and announced it was time for Autumn's mom to be seated and for Autumn to position herself to walk up the aisle.

Her parents scurried out, along with the wedding planner and suddenly Ivy and Autumn were alone.

Ivy's eyes pooled with tears. "I'm so happy for you."

"I'm so happy for me too. You don't know how close we came to losing each other twice."

"I've heard the story about the night you met." Ivy winced. "Jack told Sebastian."

"He thinks we're destined to be together."

Ivy straightened the veil beneath the glittering tiara. "I agree."

"Then let's go get me married."

They left the bride's room and headed to the chapel area. Autumn's dad, looking dapper in his black tux, walked her down the aisle.

When it came time to say their vows, Jack took her hands and smiled at her. "Autumn Jones," he said, beginning the vows he had written for the ceremony. "I think Fate saved you for me and I'm grateful. You're smart and funny and you love my cooking. But I think our adventure is just beginning."

Staring into his blue eyes, she whispered, "I do too."

The minister laughed. "Was that your vows?"

She blushed. "No." She swallowed then said, "Jack Adams, you're the strongest, smartest person I know. And I love you in a way I didn't know existed before I met you. We're going to have the best kids ever and the most fun showing them the world."

He nodded slightly, then leaned in and kissed her cheek.

The minister sighed. "It's not time for a kiss."

"I didn't kiss her lips."

A chuckle ran through the crowd.

The minister shook his head. "May I have the rings?"

Ivy and Sebastian stepped forward and the ceremony proceeded normally from there. They ate a rich, delicious supper prepared by Step Inside chefs and then danced the night away.

With their family.

And their friends.

So many wonderful people now populated his life.

Jack took it all in and every once in a while glanced heavenward, knowing his mother would approve.

Especially since he'd resigned as CEO of Step Inside and now devoted himself to creating new dishes and new menus.

Autumn had been right. As soon as he shifted back to the job he loved and settled in with the woman he adored, his life had blossomed.

He didn't think he could be happier...but Autumn's dad had told him to wait till the first time he held his newborn baby. That moment would steal his heart.

He was looking forward to it.

* * * * *

If you missed the previous story in the
A Wedding in New York trilogy,
then check out

Prince's Christmas Baby Surprise
by Ellie Darkins

And if you enjoyed this story,
check out these other great reads from
Susan Meier

The Billionaire's Island Reunion
Tuscan Summer with the Billionaire
Stolen Kiss with Her Billionaire Boss

All available now!